TRUTH OR DARE

A PARTY GAMES NOVEL

RHIAN CAHILL

Truth or Dare
A Party Games Novel

For more information visit:
www.rhiancahill.com

To my partner in crime, Lexxie, party hard!
To Heidi, for being brave and facing down not one but two
neurotic Aussies.
To the man who's partied with me for the last twenty-four years,
let the party continue.
To everyone reading the Party Games series, party on!

1

"DO I HAVE TO DO THIS?" Miki cringed at the whiney tone of her own voice.

Frankie stopped on the sidewalk and faced her. "Yes. It'll be fun, and I know it's been a while since you let yourself partake in that particular pastime."

Mikaila didn't want the talk her best friend was about to give her. Didn't need someone else telling her she'd been hiding from life. Acknowledging it herself was bad enough, but having Frankie say the words out loud would make it all too real and something she couldn't ignore any longer. With a sigh, Miki waited for her best friend to speak.

"I can tell by the look on your face you know what I'm going to say." Frankie reached for her hand and gave it a gentle squeeze. "You have to let go, Miki. It's time to start living again."

Mikaila had let go. She was under no illusions about David. The man was a selfish prick who had died too young and left behind a mess for Miki to clean up. It was the guilt she felt over *not* mourning him that stopped her from living. But Frankie

1

was right. Enough was enough. It was past time to take the first steps back into the land of the living, and a Friday night was as good as any time to start. She sucked in a deep breath and straightened her shoulders.

"Okay. Let's do this."

"Great." Frankie kept hold of Mikaila's hand as she pulled her down the path toward the house with the blazing lights and blaring music. "It'll be a chance to relive our youth."

Miki snorted. "Yeah, because that's a farce of an event I want to go through again."

"Oh, come on. It wasn't that bad. And besides, we're only reliving the good parts. The getting plastered, making out with a hot guy..." Frankie looked at Miki over her shoulder with her trademark naughty grin. "...or two."

Laughter bubbled up Mikaila's throat. No way in the world had she ever been that wild. And she doubted there was enough liquor on the planet to make her lose her inhibitions sufficiently to participate in anything that outrageous now. "I'll let you handle the making-out-with-guys part. I'll stick to having a few drinks."

"Fine. Just promise me you'll leave yourself open to anything that feels good. Don't let your brain think too hard, just feel and enjoy."

"All right, but I don't expect anything more than a hangover for me in the morning."

With a grin, Frankie turned and continued down the path, dragging Miki behind her.

MIKI SIPPED her second drink of the night and tried to appear like she was having a good time. There was nothing wrong with the party really, but she just couldn't drum up the enthusiasm needed to get involved. Frankie had abruptly taken off the minute their first drinks had been served. Strange even for Frankie, but she didn't blame her best friend. Frankie had come for a good time and, unlike Mikaila, she remembered how to have one. Then again, Francesca Winchester never stopped having fun. Miki's chest rose on a deep sigh and she leaned on the wall behind her.

The party was picking up. More people were arriving every minute and soon there wouldn't be room to breathe never mind roam around and mingle. Miki scanned the room for a familiar face but didn't see any. Things were heating up on the other side of the room, a lively game of cards had started up about thirty minutes ago, and though she wasn't sure of the rules, the point appeared to be to lose so you had to scull a drink. A smile tugged at her lips. It had been a long time since she'd played any drinking games, but she remembered them with fondness and a little pang of envy for those carefree times in her life.

She moved her gaze away from the rowdy group to take in the rest of the room. A few women talked animatedly off to the side, all of them drop-dead gorgeous and looking like they'd just stepped off the page of a magazine or runway. In the opposite corner a couple were having an intimate discussion and the rest of the crowd just seemed to be milling around. She took another sip of the refreshing cocktail in her hand. It wasn't her usual drink, but as a thirst quencher it did the job. The evening was hot, another Sydney summer scorcher, and the plain sundress she wore stuck to her front and back where a fine layer of sweat coated her skin.

Miki's gaze was drawn back to the man and woman in the opposite corner. Her eyes glued to the way he now took her mouth with a hunger that was palpable. She'd never been on the receiving end of such a kiss and a twinge of jealousy filled her chest. The woman appeared to melt into her partner as he devoured her mouth with his. Their passionate embrace bordered on indecent, but Mikaila couldn't look away. Warmth pooled in her belly, her undies grew damp and prickly heat raced over her already hot skin. Embarrassed by her reaction to the unexpected show, she felt her cheeks burn with the blush her fair complexion had no hope of hiding.

Miki was so engrossed in the sexy encounter taking place across the room that the noise of the party faded to nothing. Try as she might, she couldn't pull her gaze from the unintentional tableau. Not until her view was blocked. Two guys stepped in front of her, caging her against the wall.

"If it isn't little Mikaila Drummond." The deep voice skittered over her skin and she shivered as goose bumps broke out in its wake.

"Yeah, but she isn't so little anymore." The second voice was just as deep but slightly rougher. Both conjured images of late nights, tangled sheets and sweaty bodies.

Jeez, of all the times for her libido to wake up.

Mikaila stared at the chest before her. The tight black shirt clung to the muscles concealed beneath like a second skin. Her hands tingled with the urge to reach up and touch, lay her palms flat against that hard surface. She raised her gaze. Slowly. Each new inch she saw made her mouth drier. *Oh man.* Smooth tan skin took up were black cloth stopped and broad shoulders stretched past her peripheral vision. Miki swallowed. Blood rushed through her veins as her heart sped up. Heat radiated out from the two bodies now crowded around her, sending her temperature higher.

Arousal burst out and flooded every part of her. Need and desire that had been missing in recent years were set free in an explosion of tingling sensation. Miki took a breath, tried to slow her pulse but only succeeded in filling her nostrils with the scent of hot male flesh. Her body softened, her knees shook and she struggled to form a coherent thought.

"I think seeing us has rendered her speechless. That's something I never thought would happen."

A memory niggled at her mind, but Miki couldn't place the voice and she still hadn't managed to look at either of their faces. Her gaze had snagged on those amazing shoulders and gone no farther.

Masculine laughter that vibrated along every nerve had Miki's insides clenching. Jeez, could she be any more affected? A shiver skittered down her spine when Mr. Black-shirt placed two fingers under her chin and tilted her head up. She met a pair of startlingly blue eyes. Filled with mischief and a spark of heat, they reminded her of summer. That illusive niggle of memory flitted across her mind but refused to solidified.

"Are we that forgettable, Miki?" He feigned a hurt look that made Miki want to giggle. "Surely not."

Both men stepped closer, their warm bodies pressing into her. Mikaila turned her head to look at the second man. Green eyes sparkled, the cool colour calming, but nothing could hush the gasp that left her throat or soothe the shock blooming inside her when she finally placed her companions.

Grant Rogers and Dayne Pearce.

Oh crap. Her biggest teenage crush came back to slap her in the face. And she did mean crush. Singular. The boys had always made her feel outrageous things when they were in high school, but she'd never acted on any of her feelings because she couldn't pick one over the other. And then the summer they'd all turned eighteen she'd discovered the one thing to make her keep her distance above all else. They didn't want her to pick just one of them. As much as the idea of being with both of them thrilled and intrigued, it scared the pants off her more, and she'd walked away. Fast.

Miki closed her eyes and fought to pull herself together. She wouldn't allow those old emotions to tempt her. Wouldn't let herself fall for their charms no matter how appealing they were or how much she'd regretted not taking the chance when she'd had no real clue what it was they offered.

"The penny drops." Warm air filled her ear and brushed her neck as Dayne spoke.

"I think you're right, Dayne." The fingers under her chin trailed up to trace her lips, a light brush of flesh that sent sensations flooding through her. "Aren't you going to say hello, Miki?"

Her tongue snaked out and slid over her bottom lip, the impulse one she couldn't control. Twin groans echoed and Miki's eyes popped open to find identical looks of hunger in their gazes. An erotic thrill shook her. Her body was excited by the prospect of turning these two men on. Old desires that should have died years ago sprang to life, swamped her with their power, and moisture flooded her pussy. Mikaila's glass trembled in her hand as tremors ran the length of her body. Dear God. She hadn't been this aroused in too long to remember.

Grant stared at her, a small pout turning the corners of his mouth down. "You're not glad to see us?"

"I...I..."

"It's okay, Miki." Dayne's voice drew her gaze. "We were just as shocked to realize it was you standing over here in the corner."

"Didn't believe him at first when he said it was you. Had to stand over there and watch you for a while before the reality of seeing you sank in." Grant's finger covered her lips. "Don't say anything yet. Just come and sit with us and talk. We want to know what you've done with the last ten years of your life."

Her gaze darted between them. Could she afford to sit and

talk? The reaction she was having to them terrified and excited her, and Miki wasn't sure what talking would lead to or even if it would go anywhere. Her stomach cramped. God, did she want it to lead somewhere? Her indecision and fear annoyed her. It was just three old friends catching up, nothing more. So why did it feel like her world was opening up on a big black hole? She needed to get hold of herself. This was what getting back into life was all about. Time to pull on her big-girl panties and take the second step. The first had been coming to the party and that hadn't been so bad. She could do this, *would* do this.

Miki raised her glass and took a sip of liquid courage, nerves making her down the last half of her drink in two gulps. Licking the remnants from her lips, she took a deep breath and looked them both in the eye before she jumped in with both feet. "Okay, let's catch up."

THE CONSTRICTION around Dayne's chest eased with Miki's words. He hadn't realised he was holding his breath until it left his chest in a rush. The depth of his fear that she'd say no shocked him, but then Mikaila Drummond had never produced anything but extreme emotions in him. From the corner of his eye he saw Grant release a breath, his stance relaxing, and knew his friend was equally relieved at her answer. There were some subtle differences in her appearance since high school, but he would know her anywhere. His body knew her. He'd taken one look at her profile from across the crowded room and his cock had jumped to attention. Stupid organ had gone from interested to rock hard in seconds once his brain kicked in and acknowledged *who* he was looking at.

Back in high school her fiery hair and freckles had hidden

her true beauty from most, but not him. He'd seen beyond the frumpy clothes, wild hair and polka-dot ghost-white skin. He'd wanted to join those sexy little spots with his fingers or the tip of his tongue. Wanted to wrap his hands in her red locks and pull her close so he could take her mouth with his—still wanted to. They'd never gone beyond a simple kiss, one that had been interrupted when Grant had walked in on them. Miki had jumped away from him like a child caught with her hand in the cookie jar, and when their friend had suggested they continue and let him join in she'd run as far and fast as those sexy long legs could take her.

They'd let her go in their youth because neither he nor Grant had fully understood what she did to them other than making them horny. Years of attempting to find the same chemistry with other women had made Dayne realize he'd let the one woman who could possibly complete him—*them*—get away. He wouldn't make the same mistake twice. Reaching down, he grabbed her hand, entwined his fingers with hers. With a gentle tug, he pulled her forward. Grant slipped the empty glass from her other hand and placed it on a table as they passed.

Dayne had a clear destination in mind and quickly wove his way through the growing crowd. He held tight to Miki's hand so he didn't lose her in the crush. Not that Grant would let that happen. He was confident his best mate would be guiding her from behind. They stepped through the glass patio doors, but the timber deck proved just as packed as the house, so he detoured down the stairs and across the lawn. Scanning the area, he picked a sheltered spot near the side fence to lead them to. It wasn't dark yet but the low light of dusk would give them an intimate setting, and Dayne wanted Miki to forget everyone other than him and Grant.

Tonight they would get to know the woman she'd become

and hopefully learn all they needed to help them in their quest to have her back in their lives. Dayne had no doubt Grant would want the same thing as him where Miki was concerned, but he wouldn't count his chickens before they hatched. He'd be happy with re-establishing their friendship for now. They would take it slow. They'd scared her off before and he didn't want to risk that happening again. So the first thing he needed to know was where she lived and worked so he could find her again if she chose to bail on them tonight.

He lowered himself to the grass and pulled her down beside him. Grant flopped to the ground on her other side, his legs spread out in front of him so she was almost trapped between them and the fence. Dayne smiled, his friend was subtly making sure she couldn't escape easily. She tried to pull loose of his grip, and with the thought of not scaring her fresh in his mind, he reluctantly let her go. Cold air rushed over the heated skin where their hands had been joined, adding a startling reminder of what he stood to lose if he screwed this up.

Dammit. He shouldn't be thinking like this yet. The young Miki always had tied him in knots but this was ridiculous. Christ, she could be taken, married even. His gaze darted to her hands. No wedding ring, but was that a tan line around her ring finger? Dayne's gut clenched at the thought of her married to some faceless jerk. Jealousy and anger churned in the pit of his stomach and left a bitter taste in his mouth. It took effort, but he managed to stifle the growl building in his chest, threatening to break free.

No one spoke. The silence was not uncomfortable, but he knew it would end up that way if it carried on much longer. He cleared his throat.

"Do you want another drink, Miki?"

"No. No, I'm fine for now."

Her sultry voice slid over his nerves and fizzed in his veins.

His cock throbbed, grew thicker, and he had to wiggle his arse to adjust his pants before they choked the life out of him. Dayne glanced over at Grant and saw his friend was suffering from a similar discomfort if the bulge in the front of his shorts was anything to go by. They always were on the same page when it came to Mikaila Drummond. No other woman had ever affected them in the same way. In all the years they'd been friends they'd never shared a woman, never *wanted* to. The only one they ever craved that way was Miki. And it was a craving. Want was too tame a word for the way he felt, his need to share her with his best mate.

His gaze connected with Grant's and he was relieved to find fear swirling in with arousal in his friend's eyes. It made his own insecurity that much more tolerable. He nodded to let his buddy know they shared the same concerns. Dayne racked his brain but couldn't come up with anything to say. He had so many questions buzzing around his head, but the woman beside him had his thoughts splintering with her nearness. It was Miki who broke the silence.

"Did you two end up owning your own company? I remember you were planning to take the world by storm."

Startled that she would remember that much about them, Dayne stared at her. "You remember that?"

"Sure." She shrugged. "It was all you two talked about the last year of school."

Her neck and face flushed a lovely shade of pink, and Dayne would bet this year's profit that wasn't the only memory she had of their final year of school. "Yeah, we finally went out on our own, took us a few years to get the money together but we opened our first retail store six years ago."

"Now we have fifteen of them all over the country." Grant's voice rang with the pride Dayne was feeling. "Did you go to law school?"

"Um..." Miki ducked her head, and Dayne had a horrible feeling whatever she said next was going to piss him off. She remained quiet and he glanced at Grant who shrugged.

"What do you mean *um?*"

"I never finished." Her words were spoken so quietly Dayne had to lean forward to hear them. "No big deal, I wasn't enjoying it anyway."

"Why do I get the feeling there's more to it than that?" Dayne asked.

Mikaila laughed, the hash sound cut through the air as though she'd forced it from her mouth. "Nothing worth rehashing."

He didn't get a chance to argue the point because another blast from their past came barrelling across the yard.

"Miki! There you are. I've been looking everywhere for you."

Francesca Winchester hadn't changed at all. Still loud and full of life, she grabbed hold of Miki's hand and dragged her to her feet.

"Come on, you have to come play. You too, Dayne and Grant. It'll be just like high school all over again."

Before either he or Grant managed to utter a word, Frankie had Mikaila halfway to the house. The pleading look Miki shot them over her shoulder brought them to their feet and they jogged across the lawn to catch up with the two women.

"Hello to you too, Frankie," Grant said.

"Blah, blah. Let's go have some fun."

"I see age has matured you some, Frankie," Grant said.

"Bite me," Frankie threw over her shoulder.

Laughter burst from Dayne's chest. He could tell Frankie was just as much fun as ever, and if the things she got up to in their youth were anything to go by the next few hours would be the most fun he'd had in years.

TRAILING in Frankie's wake as she powered her way through the house, Grant wondered if he'd slipped into a time warp and travelled back twelve years. A feeling of déjà vu rolled over him, but it had more to do with past behaviour than the actual sensation of being here before. For years Frankie had led them around, often dragging them into one mess after another. A smile tugged at the corner of his mouth. Then again, a lot of those messes were hands down the best times of his teenage life.

Frankie stopped in front of a lively card game. Grant watched as a guy and a girl passed a playing card via their lips. At the last second, the guy let the card drop and planted his mouth on the girl's. Cries of "scull, scull" went up from the rest of the group, but the pair were oblivious to everyone except each other and the kiss they were currently engaged in. He never thought he was a voyeur, but his cock seemed to be enjoying the show. Or maybe it was the image currently running through his mind of him and Miki caught in the erotic embrace that had his groin filling with blood. Discretely moving so he was hidden behind Miki's back, he reached down and adjusted the unruly organ trying to work its way free of his shorts.

He glanced over at Frankie and watched as her gaze scanned the group playing Suck and Blow. If he wasn't mistaken, disappointment flashed in her eyes before she turned and pulled Miki away. They wove their way farther into the house. The crowd had grown since they'd ducked outside, and the noise level had gone up a notch too, but Frankie managed to push her way through. Passing one room where an interesting game of Twister played out, they moved on to the next. Frankie continuously looked around, searching for what, Grant couldn't say. She pulled them up at a game of Spin the Bottle but changed her mind and reversed direction before any of them could protest her choice.

She finally settled on a game of Truth or Dare. With typical Frankie finesse, she pushed the three of them onto a couch, Miki squished between him and Dayne. Two others joined the game, a guy Grant recognised but couldn't remember a name for and a woman who was already three sheets to the wind if the smell of alcohol emanating from her was any indication. Before he blinked, Frankie placed shot glasses in front of each of them and plonked a bottle of tequila on the low table in the middle of their small group. He glanced around the room to see similar groups engaged in the game already.

"I'll ask first," the other guy said as he turned to the blonde woman beside him. "Truth or Dare?"

"Dare." Her eyes were glazed and she swayed in her seat.

"I dare you to suck my cock."

"Eeww…" The blonde gagged and put a hand over her mouth.

"Jesus, Mike." Frankie poured tequila into the woman's glass before the blonde even tapped it.

With a skill that surprised him, the woman leaned forward, wrapped her lips around the top of the small cup and flipped her head back. In one swallow, she downed the alcohol and dropped the glass back on the table. She closed her eyes and shuddered before turning to Frankie. "Truth or da—" She hiccupped.

Frankie rolled her eyes. "Truth."

The blonde squinted in Frankie's direction, cocked her head to the side. "Are those four boobs real?"

Laughter burst from the group as one. Obviously she was seeing double.

"Yep." Frankie cupped a breast in each hand. "These babies are all mine."

The blonde's eyes spun around before rolling back in her head. She toppled off the seat to the floor and stayed there. Mike leaned down to fondle her chest and Frankie slapped his hands away.

"Just checking for a pulse," he said as he snatched his arms back out of Frankie's reach.

"Sure you were." She turned to face Grant. "Truth or dare?"

He thought about it for all of a second before going the safest route. "Truth."

"What's you most secret sexual fantasy?"

Jeez, she wasn't pulling any punches. He kept his gaze on Frankie. If he looked at Miki and Dayne like he wanted to there wouldn't be any point in taking the shot or opening his mouth and spilling the beans. He tapped the glass.

Frankie grinned and poured the tequila. "Chicken."

Grant ignored the taunt and took the shot. He turned to Miki. "Truth or dare?"

"Truth."

Keeping with the sex angle, he asked the question every guy wants to know. "Have you ever made out with a girl?"

Miki's gaze darted to Frankie but her head didn't move so no one knew she'd revealed the answer except him and her best friend. His mind exploded with images best not thought of and he gulped back the groan that rumbled in his throat. If anyone had seen her giveaway look they'd think she was just taking the shot instead of answering when she reached out and tapped the glass. Not about to do anything that would reveal what he'd discovered, he eased back in his seat and waited for Miki to down her penalty for not answering.

He chuckled when she picked up the glass with one hand

and blocked her nose with the other. A grimace crossed her face as she brought the liquor to her lips. Eyes scrunched closed, Miki swallowed the tequila in a rush. She wriggled in the seat next to him and placed the glass back down.

"God, that stuff is foul." A shudder rippled through her as she leaned back against the couch. "Okay, Dayne, truth or dare?"

"Truth."

"Mmm," Miki's mouth kicked up in a sexy little smirk before she asked her question. "Have you ever made out with a girl?"

For a second Dayne just stared at her before laughter erupted. Frankie snorted before joining in at the same time Grant did.

"Jeez, come on, answer the damn question and get on with the game," Mike grumbled.

"Yes, Miki, I've made out with a girl a time or two." Dayne tweaked Miki's nose before turning to Mike. "Truth or Dare?"

"Dare."

Mike almost bounced in his seat waiting for Dayne's dare. Grant thought the guy was in his late twenties, possibly early thirties, but you wouldn't guess it from the way he acted.

"Okay, how about you try sucking your own dick?" Dayne asked.

"Can't. Tried." Mike turned to Frankie. "Your turn. Truth or Dare?"

"Christ, Mike, you're disgusting," Frankie said.

"Truth or Dare?"

Grant could only imagine what the dickhead would come up with once Frankie picked her poison. He might have to take the shot on his next couple of rounds just to make the game a little more interesting because it certainly wasn't proving much fun sober, but with a haze of alcohol under his belt it wouldn't matter.

~

GRANT TOSSED BACK his latest shot. The burn of tequila seared his throat until it hit the bottom of his stomach and exploded in a ball of fire. He shook his head to try and clear the haze fogging his mind. *Damn.* He was drunk. Frankie Winchester had done it again. After a rocky start she'd taken control and turned the game around and he'd actually enjoyed playing. The woman knew how to have fun. The problem was you always paid for it later. Dayne wasn't fairing much better, but Grant's biggest worry was the woman sandwiched between them. She was plastered.

"Miki, your turn. Truth or Dare?" How Frankie managed to speak without slurring her words was beyond him. He thought she'd downed as much as he had, then again maybe not. He could only remember her refusing one dare.

"Twooff."

Oh yeah, Mikaila was plastered.

"Hey, how come you never pick dare?" Mr. Obnoxious across from them—Grant couldn't remember his name —shouted.

Mikaila stiffened beside him, every muscle taut as she sank back against the couch. He felt the shudder travel through her and heard her sharp intake of breath.

Frankie's eyes widened and, God love her, she slapped the guy on the back of the head before Grant could get up and deck him. He had no idea what the hell had just happened, but when he turned to look at Miki the frightened, freaked-out woman staring back raised every protective instinct he had. Leaning over, he shielded her from the rest of the room.

"Are you okay, Miki?"

With her blue eyes wide, she looked like a deer caught in headlights. If it were possible her normally pale skin had lost even more colour and every freckle stood out in stark relief. Grant wanted to play join the dots with his lips. Her gasp pulled him from his lustful thoughts.

"Let's get out of here." Dayne rose from the couch. "I think Miki needs some fresh air."

"Well, good riddance, she plays shit anyway."

Grant turned to growl at the ignorant prick but Frankie came to the rescue again.

"Piss off, Mike. It's not like you're the life of the party anyway with your crappy questions and dares."

Dayne pulled Mikaila to her feet and Grant joined them. Miki swayed and he steadied her with a hand at her waist.

"Come on, let's get out of here." Dayne held her hand and guided her around the coffee table and towards the back of the house with Grant close behind.

"Where do you two think you're taking her?" Frankie's voice stopped them.

"Out back for fresh air," Dayne offered.

"I think she needs to go home. If you guys will help me get her out front I'll call a cab and take her home."

"That's okay, we'll make sure she gets home safe. That way you can keep the party going." Grant wanted to take care of Miki himself, and if she needed to go home then he'd be the one to take her.

Frankie eyed him before turning her gaze on Dayne. "Why should I trust either of you to look out for her?"

Grant stared at their old friend. Did she really think they wouldn't look after Mikaila? Then again, a lot could happen in ten years.

"We'll take care of her. You have my word."

"And mine," Dayne added. "In fact, we won't take her home to her house. We'll take her to ours."

One of Frankie's eyebrows arched high on her forehead. "Your place?"

"Yeah, we live next door, Frankie. You can both crash at our place for the night then drive home in the morning." Grant held his breath and waited for Frankie's response.

"Next door?"

Grant pointed to his right. "The house on that side is ours."

Frankie whistled. "You two have done all right for yourselves then. Waterfront property in Avalon. That's gotta be worth a packet. I guess I could always sue you if you failed to look out for Miki. Or kick both your arses so hard you couldn't sit down for a week. Or break both your legs." She cocked one straight, dark eyebrow. "Or all three."

"That won't be necessary. My life wouldn't be worth living if I let anything happen to Mikaila." Grant met Frankie's gaze, the truth of his words straightening his spine. He would never forgive himself if something happened to Miki.

She gave them both one final look before turning on her heel and speaking over her shoulder. "Fine, take her to your place, but I'll be over later to check on you."

With that, Frankie Winchester disappeared into the crowd of drunken party goers.

"Wow."

"Yeah, Frankie hasn't changed much at all." Grant ginned and turned back to Dayne who all but held Miki upright. "Let's get Miki home so she can lie down before she falls down."

"I think she might need more than a lie down after the number of shots she tossed back."

"I'll put on some coffee, but it might be best if she just drank water and slept." Grant followed close behind his friend, ready to catch Mikaila if she should slip from Dayne's grasp.

Between the two of them they managed to get Miki across the back yard and into theirs. Grant slid open their patio door and punched in the alarm code. They may be willing to leave the place unlocked but not without some protection. He helped Dayne get her inside.

"Where?"

"Spare room?"

Grant led the way. The house wasn't large, but it suited them. They'd turned the fourth bedroom into a home office and furnished the third with a bed and dresser. Not that it had ever been used in the three years they'd lived here. Actually, Mikaila was the first woman either of them had brought home.

2

MIKAILA OPENED her eyes and stared up at the ceiling. Where was her canopy? The light from the bedside lamp gave off a muted glow that didn't hurt her eyes, but it did nothing to clear the fog in her head. Images and snippets of conversation swirled around but nothing made sense. The last thing she clearly remembered was heading to a party with her best friend. Damn Frankie and her need to drag Miki out of her protective shell. And where was her so-called friend anyway? Come to think of it, where the hell was *she*?

With care, Miki lifted her head and peered around the room. Definitely not hers, but the plain decor gave nothing away as to who the room might belong to. The simple wood dresser held no photos or knick knacks to offer up a clue, and the only thing on the walls other than white paint was a scenic picture of a beach. When her head didn't protest too much, Mikaila pulled herself up and rested on her elbows. Her head was all floaty, her body felt as if it weighed a ton and her tongue stuck to the roof of her mouth it was so dry.

Oh shit.

She was drunk. Or at least she had been. Now she was hung over. Had she crawled into one of the upstairs bedrooms at the party? *Crap*. She didn't even know her hosts, Frankie did. Sighing, Miki flopped back on the bed. She regretted the move the second her head hit the soft pillow and her brain reverberated around her skull like a ping-pong ball. Miki brought her hands up to cradle her head and closed her eyes. Breathing in through her nose and out through her mouth, she concentrated on stopping the pounding in her head. When it reached a manageable ache she opened her eyes once more.

The open blinds and sheer curtains revealed a dark sky beyond so it was still night. Maybe she could sneak out of here —wherever here was—and no one would know she'd taken a little siesta at all. Plan set, she scootered to the edge of the bed and sat up, her head spun a little but not enough to stop her. Her flip-flops sat on the floor beside the bed but before Miki could slip her feet into them and stand a creaking noise drew her gaze to the other side of the room and the slowly opening door. *Damn*. Escape without detection was not on the cards tonight.

Miki braced herself for a confrontation, but the slam to the gut she got wasn't what she'd expected. Larger than life, wearing only boxers, stood Dayne and Grant. Memory flooded back. The party, seeing the guys again and the outrageous game of Truth or Dare Frankie had roped them all into. Jeez, and the numerous shots of tequila Mikaila had thrown back when she wouldn't answer any of the questions. No wonder she was feeling a tad out of it. Not that she was drunk now, a little tipsy maybe but not drunk. Well, not on alcohol anyway.

Her gaze travelled over every inch of the two fine male specimens standing in the doorway. Devouring all that naked flesh in front of her had certain parts of her anatomy drunk all right, but not on booze. Oh no, lust was rapidly taking over.

And Miki's common sense and brain had been sufficiently drowned in intoxicating liquor for her to open her mouth and comment before she could think better of it.

"God, you're both gorgeous."

She spoke in a low, breathy voice that hung on the air like molten sex. No, wait. That was the scent of her arousal. Moisture coated the tender folds between her legs and she squeezed her thighs together to relieve the pulsing ache their presence had produced. The thin layer of panties and sundress were no shield against the aroma they wouldn't fail to detect if they came any closer. Neither man spoke, but they stared at her with an intensity that had her stomach flipping and her heart racing. That look coming from one man would be enough to melt any woman's underwear, but double it? Miki shuddered.

Silence charged with electricity surrounded them, held them motionless for several heartbeats. Miki's body throbbed with need. Her libido had lain dormant for so long that the sudden return to sensation took her breath. Every part of her wanted with a raw-edged desire foreign to any she'd ever known. Even in the heady first days of her relationship with David, Mikaila hadn't felt like this.

Dayne broke the spell. He shook his head and cleared his throat. His whole body shook as he snapped out of his trance-like state. Miki watched each muscle twitch as the wave rolled over him. The urge to walk over and follow the same path with her tongue was almost overwhelming and she clenched her fists in the bed cover. Swallowing hard, she dragged her gaze away and stared at the floor in front of her.

"Would you like some water? Coffee?" Dayne asked.

The mention of fluid had Miki's bladder twinging and she crossed her legs, the heated skin sticky with the slight sheen of sweat coating her from head to toe. She didn't want to think about the slick cream seeping through her panties.

"Um, can I use the bathroom?"

"Oh, of course." Grant stepped back out of the doorway. "It's straight across the hall."

Mikaila stood, the need to relieve herself more pressing now she was upright. Careful not to touch either of them as she passed, she more or less ran to the bathroom and slammed the door behind her as she entered. It wasn't until she'd finished her business that she took notice of her surroundings. The room was opulent without being ostentatious, and Miki again wondered where she was. The memory of Grant and Dayne in their underwear and Grant directing her to the bathroom made her think she might be at his house, but she couldn't recall leaving the party.

Flushed with arousal, Mikaila took a moment to calm down, but her cheeks still burned hot. She forgot about her make-up and splashed her face with water in an attempt to cool off. The sight that greeted her in the mirror when she looked up made her groan. Spying a box of tissues on the counter, Miki grabbed a handful and quickly used them to clean off the rest of her cosmetics, not that she'd worn much, a thin layer of foundation to hide her freckles, a stroke of mascara and a little lip gloss. It took a bit of effort to remove the smudged mascara from beneath her eyes, but she finally felt confident she didn't look a complete wreck and left the bathroom.

Stepping into the hall, Miki found herself faced with a wall of solid male chests. There might only be two of them, but they were a couple of the broadest torsos she'd ever laid eyes on. She stumbled back a step and both men reached out to steady her, but she avoided their touch. If either of them managed to lay a hand on her she'd be back to where she started before splashing her face with cold water and she wasn't ready to go there yet.

"Y...you mentioned coffee?" Miki's mouth got drier the longer she stared at the gorgeous men in front of her and she needed a distraction if she had any hope of controlling the urge to jump both of them.

"I did. We can have it on the back patio. It's still a lovely night and the fresh air might help." Dayne turned and led the way.

"Um..." She turned to Grant. "Is this your place?"

"Ours. Dayne and I live together."

"*Oh.*"

"Not in that way." Grant chuckled. "We were spending so much time on building the company that it was easier to live together, and then as the business grew and we could afford to buy a place it just seemed natural to purchase together."

"So, where are we exactly?" They walked into the kitchen and Miki's breath caught. "Oh my, it's beautiful."

The view beyond the glass walls was breathtaking, but the kitchen itself was every cook's dream. She ran her fingers along the marble countertop, the stainless-steel free-standing oven and the colourful tile splashback. An island bench separated the space from a huge rumpus room complete with wall-mounted flat screen that had to be at least ten feet wide. Miki had never seen a TV that big outside of a shop, but it was the ample preparation space and state-of-the-art cooking appliances that appealed to her more. What magic she could weave in here.

Miki stopped short when she saw the time on the microwave. *Two-thirty? A.M.?* It'd been barely dark when she last looked at the time. No wonder the affects of the alcohol she'd consumed were wearing off, nothing like a sleep and a few hours to sober someone up. Although she still wouldn't get behind the wheel of a car. Good thing she'd left hers at home and come with Frankie.

"Is the time on that right?"

"Yep." Dayne walked by with three mugs held between his large hands. "I'll take these out back."

"I guess I slept for a while, huh."

"You needed it. You were getting pretty drunk." Grant motioned for her to go ahead of him.

"No need to sugar-coat it. I was trashed, but in my defence I haven't had more than a glass of wine at one time in a few years." Miki started after Dayne. "Hey, you never did say where we were."

"Next door."

"What?"

"Next door to the party. Which, by the way, is still going strong. Frankie came by a few hours ago to check on you, said she'd pick you up in the morning."

"Oh, she left me here?" Miki stepped out onto the patio and marvelled at the beautiful view of the ocean.

"You were crashed out and we weren't about to wake you." Dayne pulled a chair out from the table for her.

Miki sat and reached for her mug. "I guess it makes sense that she left without me."

The guys exchanged a look that had her wondering what had gone on when Frankie had checked on her, but the aroma of strong coffee drew her attention and she took a sip. Sweetened exactly as she liked it, Miki took another mouthful before something occurred to her.

"Hey, how'd you know how I like my coffee?"

"I asked Frankie. I wanted to be sure we had what you liked when you finally woke up." Dayne took a sip from his cup.

"We weren't sure how you'd wake up after all that tequila," Grant added.

Miki groaned. "Don't mention that word." She placed a hand to her forehead. "I never want to taste that foul stuff again."

Grant laughed. "Sure thing, anything to aid your recovery."

"God, I don't think I've been that drunk in years. Possibly never."

"It wasn't that bad. Had more to do with the number and how quickly you consumed them," Dayne said.

"Yeah, kinda went overboard." She leaned back into the padded chair and sipped at her coffee. "Remind me never to do that again."

DAYNE SAT BACK and drank his coffee. It was his third. Unlike Miki, he hadn't slept since they'd come home. There was no way he could go to bed with her under the same roof—not unless they were sharing that bed and sleeping was the last thing on their agenda. The little encounter in the guest room had proven him right. One look at her all sleep rumpled sitting on the bed and his cock had gone stiff as a post. Good thing his boxers were loose fitting or he'd have suffered some damage. His limits had never been tested like they were when Miki was around. She drove his body to extremes with no more than her presence.

Even now, sitting out under the stars, every nerve was on high alert. Heated blood pumped through his veins and filled his cock. The driving pulse was a beat of sexual need he hadn't experienced in a very long time. He wanted nothing more than to strip Miki out of her flimsy dress, toss her on the table and fuck her senseless. His imagination conjured up images to torture him further—Grant thrusting between her sweet cherry lips while he drove himself deep into her tight cunt.

A shudder vibrated down his spine and his balls drew up into his body, pushing pre-come from his straining cock. Dayne couldn't hold back the groan and the rough noise slipped past his lips to echo in the quite pre-dawn hours.

"Are you all right?" Miki laid her hand on his arm.

Dayne froze in place. Just that simple touch was enough to push him to breaking point. Miki had no idea what he was thinking, what he was feeling. What he wanted to do to her. With her. *With Grant.* She would probably run screaming into the night if she knew how close she was to being ravished. And that's what he was afraid of. He wanted her so badly that he wouldn't be gentle—couldn't be.

Grant leaned forward. "Miki, you need to remove your hand from Dayne's arm."

"What? Why?" She turned to look at his friend.

"Because if you don't he's gonna lose control and I'm not sure I can stop him if he does."

"Lose control? I don't understand, Grant."

She turned her confused gaze his way and Dayne wanted nothing more than to pull her into his arms and tell her it would all be okay. But he couldn't make that promise when he had no idea if things would be fine. If there was any hope of that happening he had to come clean. Needed to tell her the truth of what he wanted—what they wanted. And when he did she just might dare to take a chance.

Dayne stood, dislodging Miki's hand as he did. He took a step away and drew in a deep breath. This was it, do or die. Truth *and* dare.

"Miki, I'm on a short fuse where you're concerned. I've always wanted you. I've never hidden that fact, but now the want is more potent, more adult, and if you touch me again I'm afraid I'll snap and not be able to hold anything back." Her eyes widened as he spoke and her hands shook as she twisted them together in her lap, but she didn't run. "It's time for our own game of Truth or Dare, Miki."

She darted her gaze between him and Grant. He was relieved to see his friend just as tense. Dayne was rushing things, he knew that, but he couldn't stop himself. Couldn't deny the primal urge to claim her as his—*theirs*—even though moving this fast could cost them everything.

"A game?"

"Yes. We're going to tell you the truth and then I'm going to dare you to do something with it."

"I'm not sure I understand."

"Just listen to him, Mikaila."

She turned to Grant, but before she could speak he cut her off.

"Please."

Dayne had never heard that tone in his friend's voice before. The word was a desperate plea for her to give them what they asked for and he could only hope she did.

"Okay."

Her answer was no more than a shaky whisper, but in the quite night it sounded like a gunshot going off. Dayne's shoulders sagged with relief, but he knew this was only the first battle in what was rapidly turning into a fight for his life. Because he suddenly knew without a doubt that Miki was the woman for him and he couldn't see any future without her and Grant in it.

"I, *we*, want you. In every way possible and more."

He watched her chest rise as she sucked in a breath. Her gaze drifted away from his and he wanted to reach down and lift her face up until her eyes met his again, but he wouldn't.

"You need to understand this isn't about just one of us, Miki. We both want the same thing. You. Together." Grant shifted in his chair so he could look at her.

Dayne crouched down beside her and took her hand. The move was guaranteed to set his nerves on edge but he couldn't resist that small contact. "We need you to understand this isn't only about sex either. Sure we want that and plenty of it, but we want more. How that's going to work I don't know, but I can't imagine being with you without Grant being with you too."

"So you two would..." she gestured with her free hand, "... you know."

He shook his head.

"Oh."

"It's just you. Without you this need to share doesn't exist."

Grant's words explained it perfectly, because without Miki the urge to share *didn't* exist. Dayne stood, pulling her up with him. He let go of her hand and took a step back.

"The truth is we want you for more than one night, but if one night is all you're willing to give us then we'll take it."

"I don't know if I can."

"I dare you to take a chance, Mikaila. One night of guaranteed pleasure with no strings attached. If you want to walk away when it's over we won't stop you." Dayne knew they were rushing things, knew they were pushing, but he couldn't slow down now. Miki made him do and say things no one else did. Made him lose control.

"We won't like it, but we'll respect that it's your choice to make just as doing anything is." Grant stepped over to stand beside him. "What happens now is up to you, but I vote we go inside and talk no matter what you decide."

"Talk?"

"Yeah. We need to know what that tan line around your wedding finger means for a start," Dayne said.

~

MIKAILA SLID her right hand over her left to hide the mark

that refused to fade. She'd worn a ring for seven years, and when she'd finally removed the gold band from her finger the obvious indent and lack of colour left behind stood as a silent reminder of what she'd foolishly allowed herself to believe. She didn't expect all trace to disappear overnight, but it had been eight months now and still the slightly lighter skin was noticeable.

She sighed. The thought of telling Dayne and Grant the gory details of her failed marriage made her sick to the stomach. But she couldn't deny her body's desire to take them up on their offer. There was just one problem. She didn't know if she'd be able to find the strength to walk away when their night together was over, and she wasn't fool enough to believe there was any kind of future in a three-way relationship. Hell, she couldn't even make one work with two people. Add a third and she was bound to stuff things up.

A quick glance at each of them told her they were waiting for her to make a move. It looked like it was her turn for some truths, no matter how much they hurt. Taking a deep breath, she straightened her spine and prayed she wasn't making the biggest mistake of her life. Although after the David disaster Miki figured she'd probably used up her lifetime's mistake quota.

"If I'm going to tell all I'll need something a little stronger than coffee."

Dayne laughed and Grant shook his head.

"Sorry, sweetheart, but you're off the booze for the rest of tonight." Grant took her hand and pulled her toward the house.

Sighing, she leaned into Dayne as he wrapped his arm around her waist. Together they entered the cool interior and headed in the direction of the bedroom she'd woken in earlier. The idea of having this discussion in the bedroom sent shivers down her spine. Whether it was fear of revealing how foolish she'd been or the thought of being in a bedroom with these two half-dressed men, she couldn't say. Before she could decide, they detoured into a room with a plush lounge and a second big screen, only this one looked more like a movie theatre screen.

"Wow."

"Yeah, it's our one indulgence. Big-screen movie viewing." Grant ushered her to sit in the middle of the softest piece of furniture she'd ever had the pleasure of touching.

"Oh my."

Dayne dropped down beside her. "Yep. Best ten grand I ever spent."

"Ten thousand dollars? For a lounge?"

He smiled, his straight white teeth contrasting with his tanned face. "You bet. I don't have time to watch movies all that often so when I do I want to be as comfortable as I can get. This..." he patted the cushion next to him, "...is the Rolls Royce of lounges, and in my opinion worth twice what I paid."

"Have to agree with him on that one." Grant sat on her other side and she was reminded of earlier at the party when they'd sandwiched her between them. Her body flushed with arousal and Miki struggled to collect her thoughts, but the hormones surging through her made it hard.

The silence stretched between them, but Miki didn't know where to start to end the awkwardness. It wasn't helping having their heat surround her. Neither touched her, but they didn't have to. They enfolded her with their warmth and scent. Each had their own distinct smell and combined they were proving to be very tantalizing. She breathed deep, pulled the intoxicating aroma into her lungs and sending awareness zapping through her blood. A shiver rolled over her.

Her temperature rose and her heart sped up, the driving beat pounding in her ears. Blood rushed through her veins to fill sensitive tissue and inflame desire unlike any she'd known.

If she listened to what her body was screaming, she'd strip naked and let them have their way. But Miki hadn't been that reckless since the night she'd agreed to marry a man she barely knew. She'd allowed the rush of hormones to colour her judgement then, she wouldn't do it again without weighing up all the possible consequences. One cost was revealing some ugly truths about herself. She just wasn't sure where to begin.

"Where should I start?"

"Let's do this like Truth or Dare except we'll just use the truth part?" Grant offered.

"How?" Miki thought she knew but wanted to be sure.

"We'll ask questions and you answer them. Simple," Grant said.

"Are you married?" Dayne asked.

"No!" The very idea that she would sit here with them and be married shocked her.

"Hey, it wouldn't be the first time a married woman has played me." Dayne's words held a wealth of information without actually revealing anything.

"I'm sorry."

"For what?"

"That you were hurt."

Dayne's eyes widened before narrowing to mere slits. "I never said she hurt me."

Miki placed her hand over his. "You didn't have to. And I'm still sorry."

He scrutinised her a moment longer before Grant entered their little game.

"When did you get divorced?"

"I didn't. I'm widowed."

"Jeez. Now I'm sorry," Dayne said.

"Don't be. I would have divorced him if he hadn't gotten himself killed."

Both men remained silent, but she found each of her hands held by strong masculine ones. It gave her the courage to say out loud the one thing that had plagued her conscience since David's death.

"I'm not sorry he's out of my life and I can't find it in myself to feel sorry for him either. He was a reckless prick who got himself killed on a dare." Her voice held a trace of the anger she'd felt since the whole sordid details of her husband's death had come out. Miki couldn't feel anything but satisfaction that David had gotten what he deserved. She was just glad the woman with him hadn't been killed as well.

"Fuck. Now I'm really sorry, Miki." Dayne gently squeezed her hand.

"Damn, sweetheart." Grant pulled her into his arms and tucked her head under his chin.

The urge to cry stole through her, but Miki was over crying for her fucked-up life. She'd done more than enough of that over the last few years. It was time to take charge and get back on track. Starting with these two men and the promise of one night of pure pleasure in their hands.

"Take me to bed."

GRANT'S WHOLE BODY TENSED. His grip on Miki tightened and she squeaked in protest. He loosened his hold and took a deep breath, his gaze connecting with Dayne's. The emotions swirling in his friend's eyes mirrored his own. Shock, confusion. Need.

"Um, Miki, as much as I'd love to race you off to the bedroom right this second you have to be sure this is what you want." Dayne found words quicker than Grant's lust-addled mind could.

"I'm as sure as I'm going to get." Mikaila pulled from his embrace and stood. "I don't know what will happen in the morning or why I want something so out of my normal conservative ideals, but I want both of you. Tonight."

Grant's cock tented the front of his boxers so he couldn't hide the way he was feeling, but he shifted so it wasn't as in-your-face. He wasn't convinced Miki understood what they wanted from her. "Miki, Dayne told you earlier what we want. We want far more than one night with you, so you can bet your sweet arse I'll use everything in my power to convince you one night isn't enough for any of us."

He pushed from the lounge and stood in front of her. "I want to fuck that cherry-red mouth while Dayne fucks your tight pussy." Grant leaned in close. "I want to fuck your arse at the same time Dayne fucks your cunt. And I want to do it over and over again. Can you handle that?"

Her eyes dilated and her breathing grew choppy so he knew his words got to her, but would she dare go through with it?

"Have you done this before?" She searched his gaze with hers.

"No. We've never wanted to share anyone but you, Miki."

She swung her gaze to Dayne who now stood beside him.

"Grant and I are close. Really close, but we've never felt this way about anyone else. It's you, Miki. You're the only one who brings out this need to share with Grant."

The silence stretched between them like an invisible rubber band pulled tighter and tighter. Grant held his breath, his heart pounding in his ears, as he waited for Miki to run. He didn't dare hope she'd agree to their demands now they'd detailed them so clearly.

"Okay, I want to be the one you share."

Relief and excitement, quickly followed by unease, rushed

through Grant as he let out his breath. If they were going to do this, make this work beyond one night, they had to be honest about everything. It wouldn't work otherwise. It seemed they were going to be playing Truth or Dare all night.

"There's one rule."

"Rule?"

"Yes. You hold nothing back and that includes your fear. If it doesn't feel good or you're unsure you say so and we stop. Re-evaluate. Understand?"

She nodded, but Grant wanted to hear her say it.

"Out loud, I want to hear the word, Miki."

"Yes, I understand."

"Good. Now strip."

Her gasp of surprise sent fresh longing through his veins, and he leaned in to taste her breath. He took her mouth with savage intent, thrusting his tongue deep to claim what would be his. She moaned and the sound caught between them as he stroked over hot moist flesh. Their tongues duelled until he'd coaxed hers out and sucked it hard. His hands found their way to her face and framed it, holding it in place so he could take what he wanted. It wasn't enough.

Grant broke the kiss and stared into her dilated eyes. "I want you naked. Now." He let her go and stepped back.

Dayne stood beside them, panting hard as though he'd been the one kissing Miki. His friend lunged forward, placing his mouth where Grant's had just been. Dayne devoured her. The sight of the two of them together had Grant's cock pulsing and pre-come oozing from the tip. *Damn.* That was the sexiest thing he'd ever seen, and he'd watched some pretty dirty porno flicks in his time.

"Jesus, let her go. I want her out of these clothes." Grant stepped around them to the back of Miki and grabbed the zipper on her dowdy dress. He yanked it down all the way, exposing the smooth, creamy skin of her back. The temptation to lick her freckles was too much, so he bent forward and trailed his tongue the length of her spine. A moan slipped from her lips and he realised Dayne had let her loose.

He stepped back and looked over her shoulder at his friend. They each grabbed a strap on her dress and pushed it down her arms. The thin material floated over her body and pooled at her feet, leaving her standing there in a matching bra and panties set. Lace the colour of ripe peaches covered her hips and arse. A thin strip crossed her back. Grant swallowed, the sight of all that gorgeous flesh barely hidden had his cock jerking in his boxers and splashing the front with a large wet patch.

Grant couldn't help himself, he reached down and palmed her arse cheeks. The soft curves were warm beneath his hands. He plumped them, squeezed and groped until she moaned again. His fingers dipped lower, pushed the fabric of her panties into the crease and gave himself a tantalising glimpse of the heat to be found between her legs.

Miki arched her back, shoving her arse into his grip while thrusting her breasts into Dayne's hands. Grant watched his friend tweak her nipples through her bra. They hardened, poked at the cloth covering them, and he wanted to take one into his mouth. He wanted to lick and suck every part of her. Taste and tease them all until they came together in a fiery climax. And he wanted it now.

"Bedroom. Now," he growled.

He grabbed Miki's waist and pulled her away from Dayne. Walking her in front of him, he steered them from the room and down the hall. Grant stopped, unsure where it was they should take this.

"Your room, it's got the bigger bed and I think we're gonna need plenty of room to move around." Dayne flung open the door to Grant's bedroom and they surged inside.

The oversized bed dominated the room. His grandfather had made the headboard and foot rail by hand, and Grant had been thrilled to receive it for a house-warming present. He was glad he'd never brought another woman to the house before. It pleased him to know Miki would be the first to share his bed.

Grant tumbled her onto the high mattress and she quickly turned and scrambled to the middle of the bed. He stood on one side while Dayne stalked to the other. Pleased to see his best friend was also breathing hard, Grant slid his hands into his boxers and pushed them off, revealing his erection. Dayne removed his underwear just as quickly and they crawled onto the bed at the same time. Miki's gaze darted between them as though she wasn't sure who to keep an eye on more, which one would reach her first. It didn't matter who got there first, they both planned to have her.

He placed one hand on her stomach and her breath hitched and her muscles tensed at his touch. Her creamy skin, laced with freckles, was like silk under his fingertips. One of Dayne's hands cupped a breast, the tip still hard from his earlier attention, and Grant remembered what he'd wanted to do. Leaning forward, he wrapped his lips around her right nipple through her bra and sucked hard. She bucked off the bed and her fingers tangled in his hair as she pulled him closer. He looked up to see Dayne giving her other breast similar treatment and the image drove his arousal higher.

His hand continued to caress her stomach, moving ever closer to the juncture of her thighs and the sweet heat waiting within. He slid his fingers beneath the elastic waist of her undies and tugged. She raised her hips and Grant grabbed a firmer hold and pulled the lace confection from her. Without letting go of her nipple, he turned his head to see Dayne's hand on the other side of her underwear, and together they removed the garment from their ultimate prize. The scent of her cream floated up to meet him. Her legs lay slightly parted, her trimmed public hair glistening with the evidence of her need.

Grant needed to taste her. Her nipple popped free of his mouth and he trailed kisses down her stomach until he reached the red hair covering her sex. He nuzzled her hip bone, the slope between thigh and torso. She writhed below him and he pushed on further, his tongue licking out to sample her essence. The slick liquid coated her sex and the top of her thighs. *Sugar and spice and all things nice.* The silly nursery rhyme played in his head but he had to agree. She was all sweet and tangy on his tongue.

He groaned. "You have to taste her, Dayne." His tongue probed deeper. "God, she tastes amazing."

Dayne joined him and Grant moved aside to allow his friend a taste. He watched in avid fascination as his mate began to eat at Miki's pussy. Grant shifted on the bed, grabbing her knees, he pulled her legs wide and slid between them. Dayne still leaned over her hip, lapping at the cream spilling from her cunt. Reaching up, Grant thrust two fingers into her channel as Dayne sucked on her clit. She went off like a firecracker. Her orgasm taking them all by surprise.

Miki thrashed on the bed and Grant used his forearms to keep her legs pinned down and open to them. He could feel the gush of cream on his fingers as her clenching walls rippled along their length. Buried deep, he held his hand still and savoured the feel of her climaxing around him. The thought of how that was going to feel on his cock had his hips bucking and his erection dry humping the bedding.

"Jesus. You're gorgeous."

Dayne's words dragged Grant back to earth and under control. He ground his teeth and fought not to come like a randy school boy. His fingers made a slurping noise as he removed them from her body and Grant brought them to his mouth so he could lick them clean. Miki's slumberous eyes watched him as he consumed every drop of her cream. He kept his gaze on hers and knew the second her need took over her satisfaction. Good, because he wasn't anywhere near done with her yet.

3

MIKI COULDN'T BELIEVE the orgasm that had just ripped through her hadn't killed her. She'd never come that hard in her life. Every sensation seemed double what she was used to, but then maybe that was because she had two men seeing to her needs. And she did need. She needed to feel one of those hard cocks buried inside her. Needed to taste their male flesh until she drove them over the edge as they'd done to her. Her muscles were weak, but she forced herself up on her elbows and stared at the two men sitting at the bottom of the bed.

"More." The request slipped from her trembling lips.

Twin smiles graced their mouths and Miki couldn't help but smile back. With a predatory air, she raised her arse from the bed and wiggled her hips.

"So who's going to fuck me first?"

Where this wanton vixen came from she didn't know, but she wanted to embrace her for one night. When neither of them moved she made the decision for them.

"Grant, I dare you to fuck me. Dayne, I dare you to come up here so I can suck on your cock."

Damn, she'd never talked like this in bed before. Never had the nerve to ask for what she wanted and certainly hadn't had the urge to direct things. Whatever it was that was going on inside her, Miki liked it. Liked the way the guys' eyes dilated and their nostrils flared when she told them what she wanted. She liked the feeling of being in control. And she loved the way they looked at her as though they wanted to eat her alive. She grinned, whipped off her bra and lay back down.

"Come and get me, boys." Miki smiled at them and spread her legs wider. "I dare you."

Grant jumped off the bed and raced to the bedside drawers. He retrieved a handful of foil packets and tossed them on the bed next to her. Dayne crawled up her body until he was straddling her face, his cock inches from her mouth.

"No, not like that." Foil crinkled as Grant got ready. "I want to watch you suck him while I'm fucking your cunt."

Miki's womb clenched. The raw words Grant used ramped up her arousal. Dayne moved to the side and she turned her head to take him. She breathed in his scent, the hot male smell driving her closer to madness. Lashing out with her tongue, she scooped up the pearly drop of come glistening on the crown. He jerked against her lips, spreading the moisture before she could lick it all up. A groan flew from his throat when she placed her lips around the head and sucked him deep.

She took him to the back of her mouth, his hard length pulsing on her tongue. Barely started, Miki lost her rhythm when Grant raised her legs and lined his cock up with her opening. With one thrust, he drove himself balls deep, stretching her to the point of pain. Her body tensed, every muscle resisting the invasion. She moaned around Dayne's cock and dragged air in through her nose in an attempt to relax.

"Jeez, you're so tight." Sweat dripped from Grant's forehead. "Am I hurting you?"

Letting Dayne's cock slip from her mouth, she shook her head. "Been a while."

"Crap." The corded muscles in Grant's neck and arms told her how tight he held on to his control. "Don't move. Just give it a minute," he ground out through gritted teeth.

Dayne reached down to play with her clit, the soft stroke bringing pleasure that masked the small amount of pain still thrumming through her. She took his erection back into her mouth, used her tongue and teeth to drive him wild. As Dayne continued to ply her nub, Miki's body relaxed and the rod buried in her depths no longer hurt. She rose up into Dayne's touch, her hips rocking and driving Grant's cock in and out in shallow pumps. Their movements started out slow and easy but soon turned urgent. Miki slurped at Dayne's shaft with little finesse and plenty of enthusiasm. It was hard to keep a steady rhythm with Grant slamming into her pussy at the same time.

After a few frantic minutes they settled into a measured pace that pushed them all closer to climax. Miki used her hands and fingers to tease any part of Dayne she couldn't fit in her mouth. And she tightened her pelvic muscles to heighten Grant's pleasure. She had both men on the verge of coming and the burst of power that knowledge gave her was exhilarating. Their orgasms were in her hands. *She* held the key to their enjoyment and she revelled in that control.

Dayne's fingers never left her clit and Miki found herself rapidly climbing up the peak again. She wouldn't have thought it possible yet, but with Grant's cock pounding into her core, the taste of Dayne's pre-come on her tongue and his skilled touch on her clit, she soon discovered she was wrong. The balls in her hand pulled tighter and she knew Dayne was just as close to the edge as she was. She wrapped her legs around Grant's thighs and surged up, slamming their hips together with each thrust.

Grant's hands slid under her arse and tilted her pelvis, the change in angle meant he struck her G-spot as he ploughed into her. Her pussy walls convulsed with the first waves of her climax. Grant groaned and thrust faster. Harder. Sensation splintered and Miki flew apart, her cry muffled by Dayne's cock as he stroked in and out of her mouth, his fingers now tangled in her hair, digging into her scalp. He continued to drive his pulsing length between her lips as she rode out her orgasm. Grant rammed deep, held still and yelled her name as he came inside her.

Miki turned her attention to Dayne, the only one of them still on the other side of bliss. She sucked hard, rolled her tongue over the sensitive crown and squeezed his balls. His sac drew up and throbbed against her fingers a second before hot jets of sperm hit the back of her throat. He shouted her name as he emptied his seed into her mouth. Mikaila swallowed, determined to take every drop. When the last spurt left his cock, he slipped from her lips with a small pop and collapsed onto the bed beside her.

Panting for breath, Miki closed her eyes and flopped back on the pillow. Grant crawled up beside her. She didn't know when he'd slipped free of her body and removed the condom, but he pulled her into his arms, her back to his chest. Dayne stretched out next to her and rolled onto his side to cover her front with his. They held her sandwiched between them and she couldn't think of anywhere else she'd rather be.

Satisfaction thrummed in her veins, the pleasure they'd delivered out of this world, and judging by the hardening cocks on either side of her it wasn't over yet. She wasn't sure she had the strength for round two, or would that be round three? First she wanted to lie here, surrounded by their solid bodies, and bask in the afterglow of sensational lovemaking. No, not making love, having sex. This was just sex. It couldn't be anything more. But Miki had a suspicion the other emotion flooding her was contentment.

DAYNE BURIED his face in Miki's neck and breathed in her scent. His cock jerked and filled with blood as the intoxicating aroma that was all Miki saturated his system. Her softness pressed against him sent another jolt of lust into his rejuvenating erection. She'd given him the best blow job of his life, but it had nothing to do with skill and everything to do with who was delivering the erotic act. Looking down and seeing her lips wrapped around his cock had been a fantasy come to life.

It still seemed surreal to him, to be lying here with her. To be sharing her with Grant. He'd be lying if he said he hadn't dreamed of this moment, hadn't fantasised about it. In his youth his fantasies about Miki had been simple, pure novice-level imaginings, but as he'd aged and learned pleasures he'd never imagined, those ideas had bloomed into some downright dirty visions. He wanted to do so many things to Miki, *with* her. Things most people would consider depraved. Take what they'd just done. Very few ever had the opportunity or the guts to do what had just transpired on Grant's bed.

Blood surged into his cock as his mind flicked through his mental album of positions he'd collected over the years. All of them starring Mikaila. He was a prick to admit it, but he'd found himself pretending more than one bed partner had been her over the years. And now he had her right where he wanted her. Well, not quite. But he'd soon fix that. He reached behind him and felt for one of the many packets of condoms Grant had thrown on the bed earlier. His fingers curled around foil and he brought the protection up to his mouth. Clamping it in his teeth, he tore it open as he pulled away from Miki.

Lying on his back, he quickly took care of business, his cock pulsing in his hand when he smoothed the latex on. Dayne reached over and grasped her waist. Lifting her from the bed he brought her over his body, Grant helped him, guiding her hips until she was poised above his throbbing erection. Miki wrapped her fingers around his length and lined the head up with her cunt. Slick heat enveloped him. Her tight hole fluttered as she lowed onto him and he thought he might lose it before he even got inside her.

Inch by inch she took him in. Her pussy felt tight, almost too tight, even though Grant had fucked her senseless only minutes ago. He wouldn't last long. The hot glove of her body would drive him out of his mind long before he had his fill of her. She slid the rest of the way down and they both groaned as her clit connected with his public bone.

"Damn, you're tight." Dayne cupped her breasts in his hands, pushed them up and together, tweaked her nipples. "Ride me."

Grant's hands remained on her hips as she began a slow rocking motion. Dayne played with her tits, tugged hard on her nipples. Grant moved a hand forward, sought the bundle of nerves between her legs, her hips bucked when he found it. Her body arched and she rode him harder. She looked like a sex goddess. With her head thrown back, her breasts thrust forward, Grant's fingers fondling her and Dayne's cock buried in her cunt, Miki gave him a visual he'd never forget.

She was flushed all over and a fine layer of sweat sparkled in the moonlight coming through the window. Her pace picked up and she slammed down with more force on each plunge. Miki reached behind her and Grant groaned in pleasure. Then it was Dayne's turn to groan. Her fingers stroked his balls and sent him into orbit. The fire blazing in his groin exploded in a fireball of desperate need. He let go of her breasts and gripped her waist. Holding her still, he drove his hips up, slamming his cock in and out as he lost all control and came with her name on his lips.

He reared up and latched onto one of her nipples. Sucking it into his mouth, he raked it with his teeth. Miki bowed against him and cried out. Grant's hand grazed his balls and he realised his friend had pushed a finger into her arse. She contracted around him and Grant's finger pressed into him through the thin layer of her body. Her orgasm milked the last of his seed from his balls and he moaned as the final waves of bliss rolled away.

Spent, Miki fell forward, Grant following. Their combined weight pushed Dayne down but he didn't have the energy to protest, never mind move. Every limb felt like a limp noodle and refused to cooperate when his brain directed them to function. Grant pulled free of Miki's body sending aftershocks of sensation through her and Dayne. Her cunt walls rippled along his length and shot electric darts of lust into his balls. A shudder ripped loose, shaking him from head to toe, and the fire he'd just satisfied sprang to life.

"Grant. You didn't." Miki spoke against Dayne's chest, her words slurred.

"Don't worry about me." Grant moved and pulled her with him. "I've got a plan and all you have to do is lie there."

Dayne disposed of the used condom and leaned against the headboard to watch. Grant rolled her to her stomach beneath him. He thought his friend was going to fuck her from behind, but he sat back on his knees and began to pull his cock in a firm grip. Obviously their lovemaking had Grant close to coming already, because after only a few hard strokes he came all over Miki's arse. Dayne's cock pulsed as his mate began to rub his come into her supple cheeks and Dayne had to check the urge to reach over and help him. No doubt about it, this thing with Miki was going to test his limits and then some.

It wasn't that he found Grant arousing, but what Grant was doing certainly pushed some buttons. Then again, watching the two of them together had multiplied his sensations tenfold. He didn't understand the need to share Miki with his best friend, but he didn't question it either. It was what it was and had been for as long as they'd known her. Nothing about his desire for Miki had been normal. He'd lusted after other girls in his teens, but he'd craved Miki. The problem had been reconciling that need with the one to share her with his best friend. And they'd never been able to do that back in high school.

Now they had to figure out how to make it work as adults. He didn't care what anyone else thought. Dayne knew now he'd had Miki he couldn't live without her, and the last ten years had already proven he couldn't live without Grant either. The trick would be meshing their three lives with as little fallout as possible. Grant wouldn't be an issue, but Miki was another story. She'd given them a night, but could he dare hope when morning came she'd offer them more?

GRANT TRAILED his hand over the curve of Miki's hip, up along her ribs and around to cup her breast, her silky skin like satin beneath his fingers. He toyed with her nipple, plucked at it until the flesh puckered into a hard point. Leaning forward, he licked at a group of freckles on her shoulder blade with the tip of his tongue before nipping with his teeth. She moaned and moved into his caress, squirmed on the bed beside him.

"Roll onto your stomach."

He nudged her gently and Dayne scooted back to give Miki

room to lie flat. Hopping up on his knees, Grant pulled her arms over her head.

"Don't move them," Grant whispered in her ear before he laved the delicate outer shell and nipped at her lobe. She shuddered beneath him. He smoothed his hand down her back and over the slope of her arse, his fingers brushing lightly along the crease between her legs. Travelling lower, he parted her legs as he continued on his journey. Reaching her feet, he massaged her insteps until she went soft under his questing fingers. Grant could see her pussy, plump and enticing, wet with her cream, but he wasn't ready to go there yet. First he wanted to join the dots up her legs, along her spine, across her arse.

He started on her left calf and licked and nibbled, stroked and kneaded. Dayne joined in, working her right leg while she moaned and wiggled. Grant found a ticklish spot at the back of her knee and amused himself by torturing her with light brushes of his fingers for long minutes. Moving on, he rolled his thumbs along her thigh, tense muscles soon turned lax under his tender care. Avoiding her arse, he began at the indent on her lower back. Dayne was a step behind, and each of them roamed her back in perfect sync as they loved Miki with their hands and mouths.

Grant worked his way back down her body, licking at the sexy freckles he'd always craved a taste of. He cupped her arse cheeks, pushed them together, pulled them apart. A glimpse of cream-slick folds had his cock throbbing, but he'd have to wait. He wanted to drive her to the edge before he took his own pleasure at the same time he let her have hers. Dayne continued to explore her back, each of them drawing moans of pleasure from her throat with their sensual assault. The little whimpers drove Grant's arousal higher, had his own need yanking at his control.

Together they drove Miki to the peak over and over, never letting her reach the final summit. If they'd planned it, he and

Dayne couldn't have been more in tune with each other—with Miki. Her moans had turned to pleas and finally she was begging them to take her.

"Have you ever taken it up the arse, Miki?" Grant slid a cream-coated finger into the puckered hole he planned to take in the next few minutes. Her answer would decide how he took it.

"Yes." The word burst from her on a cry of pleasure as he worked a second finger into her tight rear passage.

Grant stroked her clit with his other hand, brought her to the peak again but didn't let her fall. Not yet. He wanted to be buried inside her tight body when she finally went over the edge. She lifted her hips from the bed, drove her arse onto his fingers and he knew she was ready. Grant glanced at Dayne; saw his mate was one step ahead with his cock already sheathed in protection. He held out a condom ready for him. Miki cried in protest when he pulled free of her body to put the rubber on.

Dayne thrust two fingers into her cunt and thumbed her clit while Grant rolled the thin layer of latex down his throbbing shaft. With his friend's fingers still buried in Miki's hot pussy, he brought the head of his cock to her arse and pushed forward. She was tight, but he didn't get a chance to ease off as Miki reared back and impaled herself on his entire length. The cry that flew past his lips mingled with hers and echoed around them. He could feel Dayne's fingers pumping in and out of her cunt, the sensation foreign to Grant, but a stimulation that ramped up his urge to fuck her hard and fast.

He withdrew, her muscles clenching at his retreating erection. In a slow slide, Grant entered her again, the dual sensation of her tight channel and Dayne's thrusting fingers sending fire up his spine.

"More," Miki panted. "Oh God, more."

Grant looked at Dayne, and when his friend nodded, he

rammed his cock balls deep, held her hips to his and rolled to his back. Dayne's hands guided her until she sat, arse impaled on his hard shaft, legs draped over Grant's. He moved his legs wider and Dayne kneeled between them. Leaning up, Grant grabbed hold of Miki's knees and pulled them up and back. He could only imagine the view he was giving his best friend with his cock buried in Miki's snug rear end and her cunt wide open and waiting for Dayne to drive himself home.

"Jesus." Dayne's word was like a prayer as he stared at Miki's cunt with such naked longing Grant had to look away.

"Now," Miki demanded. "I need..."

"Hurry up, man. I'm not gonna last much longer," he growled.

Dayne moved forward, his neck corded as he concentrated on easing into Miki's body. Grant clenched his jaw as Miki's arse tightened further around his cock, the hot suction threatened to drag him over the edge far too soon.

"God," Miki gasped.

"Too much? Should I stop?" Dayne asked, his voice strained with tension.

"Yes. No. Oh God, more." Miki threw her head back against Grant's chest and moaned.

He felt every inch of Dayne's length as he pushed into her pussy. When his friend was fully seated they stilled. No one breathed or moved a muscle for a split second as they absorbed the amazing sensation of being joined together. Then Miki's body clenched and Grant saw stars.

Clasped in her rear passage with his best friend filling her from the front, Grant knew a pleasure like none before, none ever imagined. He bucked his hips, pulled and pushed through the hot glove surrounding his swollen cock. In a burst of action, they surged into motion. Dayne pulling out as Grant pushed in, the rhythm hot and fast. It should have been awkward, shouldn't be as natural as breathing, but that's exactly how it felt. Their mutual needs driving them all towards the ultimate release.

Miki writhed between them, caged by their larger bodies her movements were restricted, but she made up for it by clamping down on them with internal muscles. Grunts and groans echoed off the walls and Mikaila continued to demand more. Grant's balls burned with his approaching orgasm but he wanted her with him. Wanted them all to go over together.

"I'm close," he ground out through clenched teeth.

"Me too," Dayne panted.

Grant cupped her arse in his hands, held her open to their pounding cocks. She locked her legs around Dayne's waist and Grant wiggled one hand between the tangle of bodies to find her clit. His fingers brushed his friend's cock as he surged in and out of Miki's cunt before he found the protruding bundle of nerves and pressed down. The first convulsion took his breath; the second nearly squeezed his dick off as she came with a scream. Her arse milked his length as wave after wave rolled through her.

Dayne went next and Grant was blindsided by the pulsing of his friend's orgasm, the thin membrane separating their cocks was no barrier to the spasms rocking Dayne's body. Electricity shot down his spine and exploded in his balls. He thrust up into Miki's arse and held there. Spurt after spurt of come filled the condom and he cursed the necessary protection. The urge to mark her with his sperm was a primal beat he wanted to answer more than he wanted his next breath.

For long minutes they lay joined, spent and numb beyond caring, Grant barely noticed the heavy weight pressing him into the mattress. Dayne pulled from Miki's pussy, setting off another wave of contractions inside her. Grant groaned as the blood leaving his cock reversed direction and he began to harden again. She'd turned him into an insatiable sex maniac, but even though his cock thought it was ready for another round the rest of him wanted to sink into the oblivion of exhausted sleep.

Dayne left the room and Grant, cradling Miki, rolled to the side, easing out of her arse as he did. He removed the condom and dropped it in the bin next to the bed. When Dayne returned he held a towel and two wash cloths. Grant made quick work of cleaning himself up and then helped his mate take care of Miki.

"We should shower but I doubt any of us have the energy right now so this will have to do." Dayne balled the washers and towel together and dumped them on the floor before crawling back on the bed.

Grant pulled Miki against him, her back to his front with his semi-hard erection cradled between the gorgeous cheeks of the arse he'd just fucked. Hot blood flowed, pulsed through his cock at the thought of fucking her again. But Dayne was right, they needed rest. They'd catch a few hours of sleep and start all over again. This time he'd be the one in her cunt, Dayne could take her arse. With erotic visions of Miki sandwiched between them in every conceivable way dancing in his head Grant drifted off to sleep.

MIKI ROLLED OVER WITH A GROAN, her whole body throbbed like a rock band at Big Day Out. Her mouth was dry and her tongue and lips felt swollen. Her eyes refused to open, the heavy weight of her lids too much for her tired muscles to lift. Every part of her ached like she'd been run over by the nine-fifteen train. Lying perfectly still, she tried to focus on where she was and recall what the hell she'd done the night before that might warrant such agony this morning, but the last thing Miki remembered was sitting down with Dayne and Grant—

Air rushed into her lungs on a harsh gasp.

She hadn't?

The muffled snore that came from Miki's left made her flinch. She didn't move, didn't breathe. Squeezing her eyes tight on the memories now flooding her mind, she hoped it was all a drunken dream and dared to wish it wasn't. A snore tore through the room on her right and Mikaila cringed. One eye popped open and she turned her head first left, then right, a quick glance on either side before squeezing both eyes closed so tight she could feel the sting of tears.

Oh my God, she *had*.

Her heart raced and she struggled to draw in a breath. Heat crawled up her face, no doubt the accompanying red tinge with it. Could she be any more mortified? Miki tried to calm herself. Both her bed buddies were sleeping soundly if their snoring was anything to go by, so all she had to do was slip out from between them, grab her clothes and make a run for it. Easier said than done when she had no idea where her clothes had ended up. She swallowed over the lump in her throat, and as slow as possible so as not to shake the bed, she inched her way down the mattress.

The blankets had long since been pushed from the bed so nothing obstructed her progress until she got about halfway. Dizziness stopped her. Miki gasped for air. She hadn't realized she'd been holding her breath. It was the second gust of oxygen to her lungs that threatened to bring her undone. Breathing through her nose coated her nostrils with the scent of hot male flesh and sex. Her insides clenched and moisture pooled in her pussy, seeped out to cover her folds. She licked her lips, the taste of them still on her tongue. Memories of what they'd done were fresh in her mind and sent lust licking through her veins.

Her pulse sped up with renewed arousal. How she could possibly be horny after all they'd done was beyond her, but that was the least of her worries. She needed to get out of here. Away from the enticing scent of Dayne and Grant before she did something stupid like crawl back up the bed and wake them. Wriggling until her arse hit the edge of the mattress and her feet touched the floor, Miki paused, waited to see if her movements had woken either man. When neither stirred, she pushed herself upright and looked around for her clothes.

Her underwear lay about five feet away but there was no sign of her bra or dress. Miki picked up a blanket from the mess of bedclothes on the floor and wrapped it around her shoulders. She tip-toed to her undies and scooped them up. Balling them in her hand, she surveyed the room once more before remembering they'd removed her dress in the other room. Deciding to go without her bra, she padded her way to the door and slipped out into the hall. She quickened her pace as she headed for the movie room. Once inside, she dropped the blanket and pulled on her dress and panties.

It wasn't until she reached the front door that Miki realised she had no shoes and Frankie had her house key and money. Backtracking to look for a phone, she tried not to make any noise. The last thing she wanted was to get caught sneaking out of the house like a thief. Spying a phone on the kitchen wall, she raced over, lifted the receiver and dialled Frankie's home number.

"Come on, come on. Pick up, Frankie."

After the tenth ring, Mikaila gave up and tried Frankie's cell. Again there was no answer, and when voice mail kicked in Miki hung up. What the hell would she say? *Come get me, I'm at Dayne and Grant's place 'cause I spent the morning having the best sex of my life with two men I've secretly lusted after since high school?* Frankie would probably whoop for joy and pat her on the back. Miki closed her eyes and leaned her forehead against the wall, the last twelve hours replaying in her mind. Taking deep breaths, she struggled to understand what she'd done and why she thought sneaking out this morning was such a good idea.

She'd never dreamed being with them would be so good. All her fantasies paled into nothing when compared to the real thing. There'd been no awkwardness either, their love making, no, the *sex* had been natural, as if the three of them had done it a million times before. And the orgasms had blown every other climax she'd ever had out of the water too. Everything about their night together was perfect, so why was she running this morning?

Both Grant and Dayne had told her they wanted more than one night, but she didn't know what that entailed or if she wanted to know. The thought of not seeing them again had her chest tightening and her stomach cramping, but could they turn fantasy into reality? She'd never run from anything in the past, never been a quitter. Her long drawn-out marriage was proof of that. If last night had been a mistake then she'd face it and move on. And if not, she'd deal with the hurdles that came her way, but there was no way she would be a coward and run.

Mikaila pushed off the wall and turned in the direction of the hall. It was time to tell some truths and possibly take the biggest dare of her life.

~

GRANT'S HAND on his arm stopped him from chasing after Miki.

"Don't. Give her a minute. She hasn't left the house or the alarm would have gone off."

"Dammit." Dayne knew his friend was right, but he wanted to go after Mikaila anyway.

"Let's just see what she does before we go chasing after her like a pair of lunatics."

"She's running, Grant." Dayne ran his fingers through his hair. "She tip-toed from the room like a thief in the night." He reached down and grabbed last night's boxers.

"I know, but I think it was a knee-jerk reaction. Come on, think about it, Dayne. She woke up in our bed after years of not seeing us. Add to that what we did and she's got to be freaked out. And scared." Grant was pulling on his underwear as he spoke.

"Scared? She's not the only one. I'm scared to death we'll lose her before we even have her. I don't want last night to be all there is." Dayne scrubbed both hands through his hair this time, pulling on the ends.

"You're scared?"

The whispered words had him spinning to face the door. Miki stood, barefoot but dressed. She wrung her hands together in front of her and the frightened look in her eyes had Dayne wanting to pull her into his arms and hold her close.

"Miki, you broke the rule." Grant's words had her scrunching up her nose as she tried to puzzle out what he meant.

"You promised to tell the truth, Miki. If you were scared you should have told us." Dayne stepped towards her and took it as a good sign that she didn't back away.

"I..."

He moved closer, Grant followed.

"I'm sorry." She shrugged. "I guess I freaked out a little."

Her cheeks flushed red as she ducked her head and Dayne

moved in front of her. He placed his hand under her chin and tipped her head until her eyes met his. "You have nothing to be embarrassed about. Every feeling you have is legitimate and nothing to be ashamed of. Anything we do together is real and between us. And it's beautiful, Miki. Every little bit of you we share is beautiful."

Grant raised a hand and brushed the hair from her forehead. "You're allowed to be scared, Miki. This is new for all of us."

"But I don't understand how this is supposed to work beyond one night." She darted her gaze between them.

"We don't either. We've never done this before, remember? We're all feeling our way," Dayne said.

"So where do we go from here?"

"I think we take it one step at a time, one day at a time, and first order of the day is breakfast. How about I whip up some omelettes?" Grant asked.

Dayne's stomach rumbled at the mention of food. He suddenly felt ravenous for more than just Miki. "Great idea, I'm starving."

She took a moment and Dayne thought she'd refuse their offer, but she finally nodded and let them lead her out to the kitchen. He glanced at Grant and smiled. For now all was right with his world. They just had to work hard to keep it that way.

Dayne grabbed eggs, ham, cheese and tomatoes from the fridge while Grant pulled the frypan from the cupboard. Juggling his armload, Dayne turned and dumped everything on the island bench. He washed his hands before selecting a knife from the block and pulled the grater from the drawer.

"Can I help?"

"Sure, can you work out how to use that fancy thing and put a fresh pot on?" Dayne used the knife to point over his shoulder at the coffee machine.

"It's the same as Frankie's. Where do you keep your coffee?" Miki asked as she headed for the machine.

"Here." Grant opened the cupboard above Miki's head as he walked over to grab a mixing bowl. "Anything you don't want in your omelette?"

She glanced over at what Dayne was already slicing up and shook her head. "No. I'm good with all of that, just don't make mine too big. I usually only have fresh fruit and yoghurt for breakfast."

By the time Dayne had everything chopped up, Grant had the eggs whisked and the pan heating on the stove. "Do we want toast?" he asked.

"Do we have any wholemeal left?"

"If there's none in the breadbox pull a loaf out of the freezer."

Miki laughed.

"What?" Dayne asked.

"You two." Her words came out around her giggles. "You're all domesticated."

"And this is funny how?" Grant quizzed.

"Well, look at you. Two strapping men discussing types of bread and cooking, and doing a very good job of the latter I might add."

"When we first moved in together we had three options." Dayne held up his hand, his index finger sticking up. "Eat take-away every night." He raised a second finger. "Starve to death." A third finger extended. "Or learn to cook."

"Gran gave us cooking lessons. Just the basics, and we've learned from there. Although it's not that hard once you know what's what in the kitchen," Grant added.

"Do you know how to clean up too?"

"Who else do you think cleans up around here?" Dayne asked.

"I thought maybe you conned the women you feed into doing the clean up."

Dayne and Grant both stopped what they were doing and stared at her.

"We've never cooked for a woman before," Dayne said.

"You're the first woman we've had stay over, Miki." Grant's words made it clear what this morning meant.

Her eyes opened wide and her breasts rose with the breath she sucked in. "Never?"

"No," they said in unison.

"But..."

Dayne shrugged. "Never wanted to bring a woman here before now and you know we've never shared a woman but you."

"This is all so...strange." She slid onto a stool on the other side of the island from Dayne.

"Strange good or strange bad?" he asked.

"Oh, good." Miki rested her elbow on the counter and propped her chin on her hand. "I guess strange is the wrong word. Maybe I should say it's different, unusual, because it doesn't exactly feel strange."

"It feels right," Grant said from behind Dayne.

"Yes. And that makes it even stranger, I guess. Being here with both of you. Having *been* with both of you. Together." She let out a sigh. "It's going to take some getting used to."

4

"BUT YOU WANT to get used to it, right?" Dayne asked.

Grant held his breath while he waited for Miki to answer.

"Yeah, I do. And there's that strange bit again. That's not normal, is it? To want to be with two guys?"

"Well, it certainly isn't something you see every day, but then you don't see people's kinks either. It's not like they walk around wearing signs telling the world what they get up to inside the privacy of their own homes," Dayne said.

"No, I guess not. But going out will cause problems."

"How so?" Grant asked.

"Well, it's not like we can kiss and hold hands in public."

"Why not?" Grant was shocked that Miki would think they had to restrict their physical affection in front of others. He wanted to be able to grab her hand or kiss her lips whenever the hell he felt like, wherever the hell they were.

She sat up, her eyes wide with shock and confusion. "You can't seriously think no one is going to notice me holding hands with two guys? Kissing two guys?"

"Miki, we're gonna want to hold your hand some times, and

it won't matter where we are, if we want to kiss you we will."
Grant held up a hand. "Before you freak out, we're not planning to jump your bones in public and we certainly don't want
to make you feel uncomfortable or draw attention, but we also
don't want to hold back just because someone might notice. I
don't care who knows I share you with Dayne. It's none of their
business."

"You're not the one they'll look down on, Grant. It'll be me.
I'm the woman, so I'll be labelled a slut for sleeping with two
men."

"Do you think you're a slut for sleeping with two men?"
Dayne asked.

"God, no. But it's not what I think that matters."

"Of course it is." Grant's voice had risen with his anger.
Dayne didn't look any happier with the way Miki was talking
and obviously thinking. "You're the only one who *does* matter,
Mikaila. You and only you."

"But—"

"No buts, I don't give a rats arse what anyone else thinks or
says. The only thing I care about is that you're happy. That
we're happy." Grant gestured to the three of them.

Miki's gaze bounced between them. She'd pulled her
bottom lip into her mouth and Grant could see the tips of her
teeth cutting into the delicate flesh. He walked around the
island and stood next to her. With gentle fingers, he pulled the
lip free of her bite.

"I promise I won't do anything that truly makes you uncomfortable, but I can't promise not to kiss you. Not to touch you.
But if at any stage anything either I or Dayne does makes you
uneasy, tell us. Remember your promise. Hold nothing back, all
we ask for is the truth. Okay?"

She nodded.

"Say it," Grant demanded.

Miki's darted her gaze over to Dayne before returning to him. "I promise to hold nothing back."

Grant studied her for a minute longer before he leaned down and brushed his lips over hers. A quick kiss that didn't have time to turn into anything deeper as the coffee machine chimed and reminded him he was in the middle of cooking. He stepped away and walked back to the stove and the pan he'd left heating. The egg mix sizzled as he poured a third of it into the hot skillet. Dayne dropped a handful of each ingredient into the mixture and Grant kept careful watch over the omelette so it didn't burn.

The bottom browned quickly and he had to take the pan off the heat for a minute or risk blackening the underside. He used a spatula to fold the omelette in half and flipped it once before he slid it onto a warming plate and put it in the oven. Working fast, he got the other two ready and switched off the burner. Grant turned to see Dayne and Miki had set the table with plates, cutlery and coffee. Grabbing the potholder, he lifted the plate from the oven and walked over to join them.

"They smell delicious." Miki leaned over to take a deep breath of the omelettes. "I hope they taste as good as they smell."

"Of course they do." He served each of them an omelette before returning the plate to the kitchen. "Anyone want a juice?"

"No, I'm good," Dayne said.

"I'll stick with coffee."

Grant grabbed a glass and filled it with juice before rejoining Miki and Dayne. He was pleased to see his best friend was already halfway through eating, but the sight of Miki taking her first bite had his gut clenching and his cock stirring. She'd cut a small portion and brought it to her mouth but she didn't eat it straight away. Breathing in she closed her eyes and moaned.

"Damn, this really does smell great."

He watched as Miki's lips parted and she slid her fork between them. Her plum-red flesh closed around the silver tines and all Grant could think about was replacing that utensil with his cock. She drew the fork out and began to chew with eyes shut. Little murmurs of delight rumbled in her throat and his hands formed fists. Blood pumped through his veins, driving lust to every corner of his being. Swallowing proved hard with a suddenly dry mouth, but that wasn't the only thing that was hard.

His cock throbbed and pushed against the front of his boxers, a wet spot forming on the cloth. With a groan, he slumped in his chair. A glance at Dayne showed his friend in a similar position. Miki was oblivious to what she was putting them through. Her shapeless sundress hung from her shoulders like a potato sack, but those unrestrained breasts jiggled beneath it with her movements and sent a bolt of lightning down Grant's spine into his balls. He spread his legs in an attempt to ease the ache in his groin.

Miki swallowed her mouthful, opened her eyes and cut another piece of omelette. She raised it to her lips and started the whole erotic tease again. He watched in fascination, his breath stalled in his lungs, his erection pulsed and the need to be inside her clawed at his gut. The chair legs scraped along the tiles as he pushed back from the table. Fingers curled around the armrests, Grant breathed deep and struggled to remain in his seat when all he wanted to do was get up, race around to Mikaila and take her mouth with his.

She looked up and their gazes collided. He watched emotions flicker over her face, swirl in her eyes. Confusion, surprise, arousal. Electricity arced between them. Her pink tongue darted out and swiped across her lips, left a wet trail in its wake, and with a groan, Grant lost grip of his control. In three strides he was beside her, on his knees, his mouth slanting over hers. His tongue thrust deep, diving into the dark recesses to demand her surrender. Miki whimpered under his onslaught but she didn't back away. If anything, she took more. Grant's hands found her braless breasts and he cupped them, stroked them, squeezed them. The need to have her bare flesh in his hands became too much and he tore his mouth from hers.

Ragged breath ripped in and out of his lungs, his chest tight with the pain of working so hard. He stood and pulled her from her seat. Dayne stepped behind her, tugged the zipper of her dress down and Grant yanked the unflattering thing from her shoulders. The very air around them sparked when her naked breasts were revealed. Bending at the waist, he sucked one puckered nipple between his teeth and onto his tongue. Miki bowed against him, thrust more of her breast into his mouth as she wove her fingers through his hair and tugged him closer.

He curled his fingers in the waistband of her underwear and pushed them over her hips and down her legs. A sweet muffled moan drew his gaze. Miki's head was turned to the side and Dayne had taken full advantage of the angle to kiss her senseless. Grant dropped to his knees and pressed his mouth to her pussy. Her scent surrounded him and her essence coated his tongue. Probing between her slick folds, he flicked at her clit. She jerked against him, her mound riding his face.

Grant held the backs of her thighs to keep her still while he ate his fill. Her flavour was like the finest wine, a mix of tart and sweet with an overlay of musk. He couldn't get enough and pressed deeper. He glanced up to see Dayne sucking at her breast, her entire nipple consumed by his friend's mouth. The sight was more erotically explosive than any porn movie he'd ever watched. His sac tightened, his shaft throbbed and pre-come seeped from the tip to soak the front of his boxers.

Miki's fingernails dug into his scalp as she pumped her hips into his face. The sexy noises coming from her flowed over him, picked at his nerves with razor-sharp edges. Her responsiveness drove him wild. There was nowhere he touched that didn't bring a reaction from her. A shiver, a sigh, a moan of pleasure. All his senses were on high alert as he concentrated on propelling her into bliss. Grant stroked his hands up the back of her thighs, taking them inwards so his fingers brushed the hot centre of her. His fingertips easily slipped through the soaked folds to circle cunt and arse.

She writhed above him, her whole body straining against his and Dayne's touch. His friend had moved behind her, held her up with his arms around her waist, her breasts cupped in his hands. Peering up, Grant could see Dayne's mouth nibbling at her neck and his fingers tweaking her protruding nipples. Miki's fingers tangled in Grant's hair, wrenched at the strands as he sucked her clit into his mouth and flicked the hard bundle with his tongue. He shoved two fingers into her cunt and felt the first tremors of her orgasm.

A harsh cry filled the air. The air was saturated with the scent of sex and sweat. Drenched with Miki. Her hips thrashed as he drove her on and her cream coated his face and hands. Strong muscles milked his fingers, clenched and released in a rolling wave that had his cock pulsating and blood boiling. Grant lifted his mouth from her sopping pussy but kept his fingers buried deep as the final ripples of her release died away. She went soft between them, Dayne's arms around her middle and Grant's hands now cupping her arse the only things keeping her upright.

Grant ground his teeth and fought his need to come, the possibility of embarrassing himself like a thirteen-year-old a near thing. Certain Dayne had hold of Miki, he got to his feet and pulled her into his arms. She rested her head on his chest, her breathing still short and shallow. A fine layer of sweat covered her skin, and as her body cooled in the wake of her orgasm goose bumps sprang up. Dayne disappeared from the room and Grant dropped into a chair with Miki cradled in his lap.

Dayne returned with his robe and together they dressed her. The arms hung past her hands and Grant folded them back to her wrists. He was rock hard but he didn't want to fuck her now. Instead he was content to hold her in his arms and finish his breakfast. The omelettes were probably stone cold by now, but they could fix that by zapping them in the microwave. Grant was just about to ask his mate to reheat their breakfast but Dayne was ahead of him. Gathering up the plates he walked over to the kitchen.

He thought Miki had fallen asleep. Her breathing had settled into a deep rhythm and she lay perfectly still against his chest. Grant ran his hand up and down her back, from neck to arse, he caressed her spine through the robe. Her hair brushed his chin and Grant dropped a kiss on the top of her head. A deep sigh raised her shoulders, rubbed her breasts on his abs, her nipples pressing into him. His cock jerked at the erotic caress but he was determined they finish breakfast before seeking his own satisfaction. And he knew just where he'd be doing it too. Once they'd eaten it would be time for a cleanup and it wasn't just the dishes that needed a wash.

MIKAILA KNEW she should get up. But after the orgasm Grant and Dayne had just given her she could barely lift her head, never mind stand on her own two feet. Her bones felt like melted chocolate, all warm and soft. Every inch of her skin tingled and she had pins and needles in her fingers and toes. The throbbing ache in her breasts and groin were a constant reminder of the mind-numbing pleasure these two men had delivered. Again. She'd be lucky if they didn't kill her. Actually, she'd be damn lucky to die at their hands.

She took a deep breath and let it out slowly. Grant sat quietly, his hand sweeping up and down her spine in a soothing rhythm that would soon put her to sleep. Dayne was banging things around in the kitchen, but the noise sounded far away to her fogged senses. Miki snuggled into the plush robe they'd dressed her in, the soft material smelled of Dayne and sunshine. With her eyes closed, she relaxed into Grant's warm embrace and let the beating of his heart lull her into that space between wake and sleep.

Grant shifted underneath her and the press of his erection into her thigh sent arrows of need into her core. Would he always affect her this way? Neither of them could touch her without her body reacting. Overwhelmed by her continuous arousal, Miki pushed up and tried to get off his lap.

"Uh-huh, stay here. Dayne is reheating the omelettes so we can finish breakfast." Grant tightened his arm around her waist.

"I can't sit on your lap to eat."

"Yes, you can." Dayne put a plate in front of them. Picking up a fork, he broke off a piece of omelette and raised it to her mouth. "Open up."

"You—" Miki had no choice but to take the offered food. While she chewed Grant used his free hand to feed himself before getting a second bit ready for her. She opened her mouth to protest as she leaned over to grab a fork of her own, but Dayne snatched the utensil out of reach and Grant fed her another forkful of egg. Chewing quickly, Miki swallowed the mouthful and spoke in a rush before either of them could shove more food down her throat. "You know I am capable of feeding myself."

"Yep. But it's kind of nice taking care of you like this," Dayne said as he offered her more.

She flattened her lips, determined to stop him. But they were just as adamant to get their way. Together they initiated a sneak attack. Grant tickled her ribs and the second she gasped Dayne pushed the food past her lips.

"Hey. No fair," she spoke around the omelette.

Dayne grinned as he forked some into his own mouth.

"You need to eat and we want to feed you. Seems a simple enough thing to me," Grant said.

"Spoon feeding me is simple?"

"Actually, yes. See?" Dayne scooped up some more egg and brought it to her lips. "Open wide."

Miki rolled her eyes. "I'm not two you know." She opened her mouth and took the food.

"No." Dayne looked down at her breasts where they were partially visible between the crossed lapels of the robe. "You're *definitely* not two."

Banked fire smouldered in Dayne's eyes and an answering warmth flared in the pit of her belly. She squirmed on Grant's lap as she squeezed her legs together in an attempt to ease the throb. The move dragged a groan from his chest. Grant tossed his fork on the table and placed his hand on her leg just above her knee, his fingers digging into her muscle.

"Had enough?" The rough, gravelly sound of his voice shivered over her skin.

Dayne put his fork down and stood. The flames in his gaze burned brighter and he offered her a hand. "Come on. Time to clean up."

Grant's hand moved to her lower back and with a gentle push, he helped guide Miki to her feet. Her legs were like jelly, wobbling and threatening to give way, but she didn't get a real chance to test them before Dayne bent his shoulder to her stomach and lifted her off her feet.

"Hey!"

He patted her arse. "Relax. Let us do all the work."

Relax? He had her slung over his shoulder like a wet towel, how was she supposed to relax? "And what exactly are we doing?"

"Cleaning up."

Miki raised her head to look at Grant walking behind them. "Cleaning up?"

"Yep, time for a shower." His sexy grin curled her toes and sent heat spiralling through her belly.

They entered Grant's room and Dayne put her on her feet. Her head spun and she took a second to steady herself. Grant made his way to the bathroom Miki could see through the open door on the other side of his big bed. Dayne gripped her hand in his and tugged her across the floor.

"Come on."

Grant's bathroom was spacious. Large white tiles covered the walls with a row of smaller colourful ones running around the room at chest height. The toilet was tucked in behind the door and a vanity ran the length of the wall. At first Miki thought there wasn't anything else in the room, but the far wall didn't meet one side and the gap was big enough to walk through. Grant disappeared behind the half-wall and it soon became obvious what was hidden behind it.

The sound of rushing water echoed off the tiles and steam quickly billowed out into the main area. Dayne slipped the robe from her shoulders as Grant reappeared. Both men stripped out of their underwear and led her back into the shower alcove.

"Turn around," Grant directed.

Turning, Miki let him push her back a step and warm water cascaded down her back. She moaned as the spray hit stiff muscles, relieving tension she hadn't realised was there. Relaxing, Miki closed her eyes and tilted her head back. The hot stream beat against her scalp and soaked her hair. Slippery fingers stroked over her shoulders and down her arms. Lifting her eyelids, she saw Dayne had lathered his hands and had begun to wash her. He wove his fingers between hers, his face a mask of concentration as he took his job seriously.

"Is this going to be like the feeding thing?" she murmured.

"Yep." Grant reached for the shampoo. "Let us take care of you."

"This is bizarre, you know that, right?" Being washed by someone else might be out of the ordinary, but Miki didn't want to make them stop. It felt way too good having those soapy hands on her body and in her hair.

"No more bizarre than finally getting you where I want you," Dayne said.

"Oh? And where's that?"

"Between us." He nodded at Grant behind her. "Naked." His sexy grin said it all. The man loved every second of having her between them.

Miki let out a sigh as Dayne's slick hands roamed down her chest and Grant massaged the shampoo into her scalp. "God. You're so good at this. Had much practice?"

Grant chuckled. "Only on myself."

"You're the first," Dayne added.

Her insides warmed and if she'd been born over a hundred years ago their words would have made her swoon. As it was she was close to pooling at their feet under their sublime ministrations. Dayne's hands were on her breasts. Circling around and around until he reached her taut nipples. His fingertips captured the hard buds and rolled them, the suds making them pop free of his hold when he squeezed too tight. A moan slipped from her throat and Miki arched, seeking more of his touch.

"You like that?" Dayne asked as he repeated the erotic caress.

"Yes." The word ended in a moan.

"I know something you'll like better." She could hear the smile in his voice.

His hands travelled lower, over her ribs, across her stomach. Fingers strummed and kneaded. Hands gripped and cupped. Dayne explored every inch of her torso, his soapy hands losing some of their slickness as the water washed away the suds. Grant continued to weave his magic fingers through her hair, his short nails grazing her scalp and sending shivers down her spine. He tilted her head back farther and directed the shower over her to rinse away the suds.

Miki's eyelids fluttered closed as she fell into the sensations their actions created. She'd never felt more cared for. The gentle strokes and hard press of fingers and hands soothed, aroused, enthralled. Every glide of their flesh along hers produced a whirlwind of feelings, physical and emotional. For someone used to doing the nurturing, to have the tables turned, to be the receiver instead of the giver, was not only mind-blowing but devastating to the walls she'd built around herself.

Frankie was the closest person to her, but after just one night with these two men Miki knew they could be just as close, just as important. Her stomach clenched and her heart beat faster. She'd let a man be important to her once before and look what that had gotten her. Nothing but heartache, and she didn't think she could go through that again. No, she'd have to harden her heart, toughen up those walls and hope they held.

Dayne's hands moved between her legs and every serious thought in Miki's mind evaporated. He pressed the bundle of nerves at the apex of her slit and her pussy clenched and her legs shook. Grant, finished with her hair, brought his hands around her waist and cupped her breasts in his palms. His fingers plucked at her nipples, pinched and tugged. With a moan, she arched her back and thrust her body against their questing hands.

Gently and easily, they drove her up. Grant played with her breasts until they felt swollen and heavy, and still he kept going. Dayne slid two fingers inside her, used his thumb to keep up the pressure on her clit while pushing his other hand between the cheeks of her arse. He probed her back entrance, circled the puckered opening before pressing into the dark depths. Her hips jolted as though she'd been struck with a livewire.

The orgasm flowed over her. Like falling rain, it trickled, unhindered along her nerve endings. She bowed into Dayne, crushed her chest to his, trapping Grant's hands between them. Both men pressed against her, Grant's cock riding the crease of her arse and Dayne's grinding into her hip. Miki wanted them inside her. Wanted to feel their cocks pounding into her at the same time.

"Please."

Dayne removed his hands from her pussy and dropped to his knees, pulling her down with him. She straddled his hips, spread her legs wide and impaled herself on his erection. Both of them groaned as she sank onto his length. Wrapping his arms around her back, he held her close and lay down on the tiles. Water fell around them, the warm spray blurring her vision and making their skin slide together. Grant moved in behind her and spread her cheeks with one hand while slathering something cold and slick on her anus with his fingers.

Grant eased a finger into her tight passage, worked it in and out before adding a second. Dayne remained still beneath her and Miki wanted to move more than she wanted to breathe except his hands on her hips stopped her. It seemed like hours but could only have been seconds, before Grant slid his fingers free and replaced them with his cock. He drove into her, long and slow, he forged his way in. Tissues already inflamed from her orgasm burst with renewed sensation and the wait became too much. She bucked as pleasure erupted.

Pinned by their bodies, Miki moved little. Dayne and Grant did all the work. From below, Dayne thrust up, plunging his cock in and out of her pussy. Behind her, Grant drove his length back and forth, his rhythm opposite to Dayne's. Her knees rested on the hard tile, the ceramic digging into her skin. She didn't care. All that mattered were the two men loving her with their bodies and the pleasure they sought in her. Miki rocked her pelvis, clenched her inner muscles and squeezed their flesh in a rolling motion that pulled groans from their chests.

Their pace increased and they pumped into her together. Surging forward and retreating in short, sharp strokes that shoved her up and over the edge. With a cry, she thrashed between them, her release milking them of theirs. In a rush, they came, calling her name and burying themselves balls deep in her grasping channels. Wrapped in their arms, Miki floated back to earth, their dual embrace bringing far more than physical pleasure.

Mikaila lay sandwiched on the tile floor by two men she thought she'd missed her chance with years ago. In less than twenty-four hours she'd lived out her ultimate fantasy and couldn't regret a second of it. On the heels of that thought came another. She was falling for them. Far and fast. And no amount of internal lecturing on her part was going to save her.

~

FUCK!

She'd done him in. Dayne couldn't move, couldn't breathe. Had he ever come so hard before? Not in recent memory. He closed his eyes, dropped his head against the tile floor and tried to catch his breath. The weight pressing down on him shifted, he opened his eyes to see Grant pulling from Miki's body and moving to the side. Their gazes connected, and in that split second they both realised the same thing. They hadn't used protection.

His naked cock still lay deep inside her. The hot glove of Miki's body gripped his softening length like wet silk. He had to say something. What, he hadn't a clue, but sorry might be a start.

"Oh, God, Miki, I'm sorry."

She mumbled into his chest, her lips brushed his nipple and he shuddered in reaction. He hadn't caught the words, and when she pinched his stomach he jumped, yelping with the sharp sting.

"Hey!"

Miki raised her head, rested her chin on her hand and stared at him. "You did not just apologise for giving me a mind-blowing orgasm did you?"

"Ah, no." How the hell was he going to say he'd screwed up as monumentally as he had? Sure, Grant had fucked up royally too, but it was his come that could get her pregnant, not his friend's. "We forgot condoms."

Her eyes widened. "Did we?" Miki stilled, her gaze going from Dayne to Grant and back again. "I'm okay. There's no risk of disease or pregnancy from me."

"I'm clean. Get tested every year with my physical and I've never had sex without a condom before," Grant said.

"Same." Dayne brushed her wet hair off her forehead. He wasn't about to admit that twinge in his gut was disappointment that there wasn't a chance she'd be carrying his child. "Are you sure there's no risk?"

"I'm sure." Miki laid her head back down and sighed. The sound held a wealth of emotions but Dayne couldn't tell what they might be.

"The water's going cold. Let's finish cleaning up before we freeze." Grant got to his feet and helped Miki up.

"Maybe you should leave then, because I was looking pretty clean before you two got started." Miki's laughter gurgled in the small enclosure and Dayne couldn't help joining in.

"What can we say? Naked and wet you're just too much temptation." He dropped a kiss on her nose as he stepped up beside her and reached for the soap.

The three of them finished showering without speaking, which gave Dayne plenty of time to think about that strange feeling in his gut that he'd missed out on something. He knew what he was doing. Mikaila had always been his ideal, the type of woman he'd want to share his future with. Only it had been more than a type, it had been Miki. How he'd managed to ignore that fact for most of his adult life was anyone's guess. But now, with her here, he knew what he wanted. A life with her. With Grant. Watching her grow big with their children.

Dayne stepped out of the shower. The water shut off behind him and he grabbed a towel for each of them. He held one open for Miki to step into and he wrapped it around her. After a quick hug, he let her go and tossed a towel at Grant. With efficiency, Dayne rubbed the soft cotton over his body. In minutes he was dry and had the bath towel secured around his hips.

"I'll go get dressed. We still calling into the Manly store today?" he asked Grant.

"Yeah, we need to pick up that stock I ordered." Grant

slung his towel around his neck, seemingly oblivious to the fact he was naked. "It'll only take a few minutes though, so the rest of the day is free to enjoy."

"Um, can I trouble one of you to drop me off at home? Frankie has my money and keys, but Mrs Brimble next door has a spare in case of an emergency."

"No problem. You'll need something else to wear anyway. That dress you had on last night is a little worse for wear." Dayne smiled at her.

"Wear? Why?" She tucked the end of her towel between her breasts, concealing her body from view.

"You're spending the day with us," Grant said, the timber of his voice invited no argument.

"But—"

"There you go with those buts again. No buts, Miki. We're spending the day together." Grant strode from the room.

"Well, I guess the washing will have to wait."

Dayne laughed. "I'm sure we can make up for the disappointment." He slung his arm around her shoulders and led her from the room.

They ignored Grant as he grumbled inside his walk-in wardrobe and made their way to Dayne's room. It was one of the few rooms Miki hadn't been in and for some reason he wanted her to see it, to like it. He'd decorated in greens and blues, with dark timber furniture. He liked the room, the soothing effect it had on him after a long day, and he wanted Miki to feel the same. Her approval was important and Dayne was beginning to wonder if maybe they'd gotten themselves into a situation that none of them stood a chance of getting though without being hurt.

He wouldn't worry about it now. There was no need to borrow trouble. Better to play it one step at a time, like Grant had said, take each day as it came and make the most of everything that happened. Dayne had never shied away from hard work before, and Miki was becoming just as important, if not more important than anything he'd ever fought for in the past. The grip he had on her hand tightened and when she squeezed his fingers in return he breathed a little easier. Maybe they stood a decent chance of making this unconventional relationship work.

"Come on, you can borrow a shirt and shorts if you don't want to put your dress back on." He tugged her into his room and headed for the dresser without letting go of her hand.

"Maybe a button up shirt to go over the top? I don't think it's as bad as you two are making out, and I need to walk from car to house in it, not have lunch in a five-star restaurant."

"Okay." Dayne indicted the walk-in robe. "Take your pick."

Rummaging in his drawers, he pulled out fresh underwear, a T-shirt and shorts. He dropped the towel and quickly dressed, surprised to find Miki still in his wardrobe. Dayne walked over and leaned against the jamb. She had her back to him and was flicking through his casual shirts, discarding each one after a careful perusal. After some minutes she settled on a white dress shirt.

"Can I use this one?"

He nodded. "If that's the one you want."

"I guess my dress is still in a crumpled heap on the dining room floor." She slipped the shirt from the hanger and returned it to the rack. "So what are we going to do for the rest of today?"

Dayne knew what he wanted to do, but he didn't think Miki would go for a day spent in bed and they had to go pick up the stock Grant had ordered. "I'm not sure. Grant mentioned lunch in by the harbour."

"Dressed like that?" Miki indicated his shirt and shorts.

"There's plenty of places to eat that don't require a suit and tie, Miki," Grant spoke behind him. "Here, I brought your clothes."

Miki took the bundle from Grant's outstretched hand and waited.

"Aren't you going to get dressed?" Dayne asked.

"When you two leave the room."

"Miki, honey, we've seen you naked," Grant said.

"That may be, but undressing in the heat of the moment is a lot different, and I'd prefer to dress in private."

Dayne wasn't sure laughing at her was a good move, even if he did think it was funny to hide from them after everything they'd done, so he clamped his lips shut and backed out of the small room. "Okay, we'll wait in the kitchen."

He curled his fist in Grant's shirt and pulled him backwards. Neither of them took their eyes off Miki and it wasn't until she shut the wardrobe door in their faces that Dayne let his laughter free.

"What the hell was that about?" Grant asked as they turned and left Dayne's bedroom.

"Hell if I know. It seemed completely out of place after everything she's let us do." He shrugged. "But at the moment I'm willing to do almost anything to keep that woman happy."

Grant sighed. "Me too."

They entered the kitchen and Dayne groaned when he saw all the dirty dishes still sitting on the table. "Crap. I forgot about this mess."

"Shit. Guess we could clear it up while we wait for Miki."

"Seems like a good idea. Especially seeing how we told her we could cook *and* clean."

Dayne began stacking plates while Grant grabbed coffee mugs. Together they made quick work of scraping the leftovers into the bin and loading the dishwasher. When Miki walked in,

Dayne was giving the table a wipe down and Grant was throwing out the stale coffee. Glancing up, he froze.

She'd put his shirt on over the top of her dress, and instead of doing up the buttons she'd tied the sides at her waist. He swallowed over the lump in his throat. The sight of her in his shirt did weird things to his insides, but what really made him come undone was the image of her in nothing but his shirt that flashed in his mind. He'd have to remember to get her to wear it like that later. His cock hardened, pressed against the fly of his denim shorts. *Damn.* The bloody shirt wasn't the only thing tied in knots.

5

MIKI LAY on the hot sand and dug her fingers into the fine grains. She couldn't move. After stopping by the C.S. store in Manly they'd headed into Sydney and had lunch in Darling Harbour. They'd eaten at a Thai restaurant, where her taste-buds had been subjected to the most exquisite food she'd ever eaten. Having never really had true Asian food before, she'd let the guys order for her, and boy was she ever glad she had. Her mouth still tingled from one of the spicy dishes but the flavours of each meal they'd sampled were amazing.

"I don't think I can move," she murmured.

"Me either, and I didn't eat as much as you," Dayne said.

She turned her head towards him. "You ate more!"

"Not if you do the whole percentage consumed to body weight thing."

"What?"

"I outweigh you by at least double, so I get to eat twice as much." He gave her a cheeky grin. "And there's no way I came close it eating two times what you packed away."

At a loss for words, Miki's mouth flapped like a fish out of water. Then Dayne started to laugh. A belly-deep, gravelly sound that flowed over her like a warm summer breeze. Her insides heated and churned as arousal began to simmer. All through the day she'd managed to keep her sexual hunger for them at bay. Managed, barely, to ignore the urge to touch and kiss. She hadn't wanted to draw any unwanted attention and until now it wasn't a problem.

Now she wanted to lean over and kiss those laughing lips. Wanted to dip her tongue inside his mouth and taste him.

"Do it."

Her gaze darted to his.

"I can see it in your eyes, Miki. I know you've been holding back. Come on. I dare you."

Miki wasn't sure what shocked her more. The fact he could read her so well or that she wanted to take his dare.

Grant ran a fingertip down her arm. "Go on, Miki, kiss him like you want to, like you mean it."

She licked her lips, the moisture cooling in the soft breeze. Dayne groaned and leaned closer. Their mouths were inches apart but Miki could feel his heat, taste his breath. With a sigh, she gave in to the craving. Her lips brushed his and that barest of touches set of a blaze of desire that consumed them both. His tongue stroked hers, fierce lashes that dragged her deeper. Miki rolled into him, chest, stomach, legs, pressed together, their mouths fused in a scorching kiss.

Heat exploded in her belly, dribbled down into her core to light a fire deep within. She ground her pelvis to him, her mound rubbing on his swollen shaft, the pressure not enough. Tearing her mouth from his, Miki gasped for breath and stared into lust-filled eyes.

"Jesus." She licked her puffy lips. "What you do to me."

"It's mutual, baby."

"Fuck!" Grant cursed behind her. "That has to be the hottest thing I've ever seen."

Miki glanced over her shoulder to find Grant on his side, inches from her. The muscles in his neck were corded and sweat beaded on his forehead. She let her gaze travelled down his body until it snagged on the bulge in his shorts.

"Oh, yeah. I'm just as hard as Dayne, and I haven't even touched you."

Her mind spun with the knowledge of what she did to them. Dayne was right. They may do unbelievable things to her, but they weren't immune to her either. Twisting around to face Grant, she trailed a fingertip through the moisture on his upper lip and wondered how he would taste there. Would it be salty from his sweat? Would she taste the spices from lunch on his tongue like she had with Dayne?

"Don't stop now, Miki. Go for what you want."

Grant's words spurred her on and she pushed her tongue out to lap up the dampness on his skin. He moaned beneath her and she went farther. She probed the seam of his lips until he opened to her. Salt and spice. The combination was more tantalising than any gourmet meal and Miki ate her fill. Heat covered her front as he pulled her to him and took their kiss deeper. Dayne made a strangled sound behind her a split second before he pressed his front to her back.

For long moments she indulged in kissing Grant while Dayne nibbled at her neck. Nothing but her need and the men who could satisfy it mattered. Caught in their erotic embrace, the sound of children playing barely registered until sand was sprayed over of them. Abruptly brought out of her lust haze, Miki stilled. The shock of knowing just how carried away she would have gotten without the interruption scorched her neck and face.

"Don't." Dayne's lips brushed her ear. "They're just kids running past."

Grant eased away and looked into her eyes. "Relax, Miki. We won't do anything you don't want, remember?"

She nodded. Her brain knew neither of them would push her for more, but it wasn't them she had trust issues with. Their little interlude had just given her some eye-opening insight about herself. No, she knew she could trust them. It was herself she was no longer sure of.

"Miki?"

"You promised no holding back." Dayne was leaning over her shoulder so he could see her face, his concern written in every crease on his forehead.

Miki glanced back at Grant, his face a similar mask of worry. "I'm okay."

Neither man seemed convinced by her softly spoken words but she didn't have it in her to argue her case because Miki suddenly wasn't sure if she'd ever be right again.

"Come on. Let's go build sandcastles." Dayne got to his feet and offered her a hand.

"Sandcastles?"

"What? You've never built one?" Grant asked as he stood and brushed the sand from his legs and arms.

"Sure but not since..." When was the last time she'd played in the sand?

"All the more reason to do it now." Dayne grabbed her hand and pulled her towards the shoreline.

"How are we going to build a castle without the proper tools?"

Grant put up his hands, waggled his fingers at her. "These are all the tools I need, fair princess."

She laughed. "Princess?"

"Every castle needs a princess." Dayne knelt in the damp

sand and tugged her down with him. "And if anyone deserves to be a princess for a day it's you."

Miki's heart turned over. She didn't doubt his sincerity, but it was hard to adjust to their caring when she'd been used to none for so long now. Frankie was the only person left in her life who cared about how she was or what she wanted. And even her best friend couldn't make up for everything that was missing in Miki's life.

"Hey." Grant placed a finger under her chin and raised her gaze to meet his. "Why such a serious face? This is meant to be fun, Miki."

"Royal decree." Dayne mimed blowing a trumpet. "The kingdom is only allowed to have fun between now and sundown, by order of the royal court."

Miki laughed at his silly accent and even sillier acting skills.

"That's better." Grant let go of her face and dug his hands into the wet sand. "Now, let's build us a castle."

"We need a moat." Dayne began digging a trench. "How big do we want this thing?"

"A couple of feet for sure."

"Okay." Dayne curved the channel he was working on.

She sat back and watched the two of them playing in the sand like little boys. They made her smile, even when her heart felt like it might explode and her mind whirled with a thousand and one confusing thoughts, they managed to take it all away and make her laugh and enjoy the moment.

"Come on, you." Grant poked her with a sandy finger. "Just because you're the princess doesn't mean you don't have to work."

Miki dug her hands into sand and scooped up a pile to add to the tower Grant was building. Slapping the wet mix against the small structure, she grinned. She patted the side and used her fingers to push it into the right shape. With each handful their castle took shape, and Miki forgot all about her worries. They had two towers and the outside walls built when Dayne's moat caused a cave in.

"Hey, watch it." Grant worked quickly to push the wall back up.

"Sorry, got a little too close there." Dayne grinned, not sorry at all.

"If you're not careful I'll have the guards throw you in the dungeon," she said. Where the frivolous words came from Miki didn't know and didn't care. It felt good to play.

Dayne gasped and placed a hand on his chest. "My humble apologies, my princess. I will strive for it not to happen again." He affected a ridiculous half-bow.

Laughter bubbled up her throat and burst free. The carefree sound was strange and unfamiliar to her ears. She pushed at his shoulder. "You're such a clown."

"More like the court jester," Grant said.

"You're just jealous that I have the princess's attention and you don't." Dayne stuck his tongue out at Grant.

The childish behaviour only made her laugh harder. Her sides hurt and tears stung her eyes. "Stop. You're killing me." She spoke between giggles.

"Never." Dayne lunged for her, tackling her to the wet sand and finding the ticklish spots along her sides.

"No. Stop. Don't." Each word was a gasp as she fought for breath.

"Are your feet ticklish too?" Grant lifted one foot and began running his finger on the underside.

"No!" She wiggled in Dayne's grasp but his grip on her was too good. "Oh, oh. Stop."

Miki laughed uncontrollably. Tears streamed down her cheeks and still they didn't stop. She was almost out of breath, the fight gone out of her when they finally let up on their attack. With a sigh she slumped in Dayne's arms.

Grant stared at her. "God you're gorgeous."

Her gaze met his. "What? Wet, sandy and probably bright red to match my hair because you two just tried to tickle me to death?" she snorted. "Yeah, right. Gorgeous like a pile of shit."

"You really don't see it do you?" Dayne asked.

"See what?"

"How beautiful you are," Grant said.

"I'm not saying I was beaten with the ugly stick, but I'm not beautiful. Passably pretty maybe, on a good day, but definitely far from gorgeous." Miki wasn't one to delude herself and she'd come to terms with her looks a long time ago.

"The ugly stick? Where the hell did you get that from?" Dayne asked.

"It's something my dad used to say when I was a kid."

"What? To you?" Grant scowled.

"No!" She smiled, remembering. "He used to say it about our dog. That thing was the ugliest little mutt on the planet and Dad used to say how his mother must have beaten him with the ugly stick."

"Just as well. I think Grant might have been thinking of committing some beating of his own." Dayne gave her a squeeze.

"He's dead."

"What? The dog?"

"No, my dad. He and Mum were killed in a car accident five years ago."

"Oh, Miki." Dayne pulled her back into his arms. "I'm so sorry; I remember how close you all were."

It had taken her a few years but she was finally over their early deaths. She still missed them like mad, but it no longer hurt to talk about them like it had in the beginning. "We were close and I have all those wonderful memories to cherish."

The mood had turned serious again and Miki wanted to get back to the carefree abandon of earlier. "Come on. This castle won't build itself." She crawled from Dayne's lap and started working on another tower.

GRANT SAT in damp pants watching his best friend and the woman he thought he might be falling in love with play like a couple of three-year-olds. Miki's face was lit up, her pale skin glowing, the multitude of freckles standing out. He'd meant what he said. To him she was gorgeous. Her red hair burned brighter under the hot sun and the tint of scarlet across her cheeks showed she'd caught a little sunburn. They hadn't thought to bring hats or sunscreen, but it was late in the day and the UV rays had lost some of their sting.

Miki's denim shorts were wet in patches, the sand sticking to them in clumps. She had her hair pulled up in some sort of clip that no longer appeared in control of the burnished mass. Ropey strands hung about her face and down her back like dark streamers. His fingers itched with the remembered feel of tangling with all that spun gold. There was no doubt in his mind she'd need to wash her hair again after today. He could see a smattering of fine yellow grains on the top of her scalp.

"Hey, are you helping or freeloading on your arse?"

He grinned at her. "Just admiring the view."

She turned towards the sea. "Yeah, it's pretty spectacular."

Dayne laughed. "Somehow I don't think that's the view Grant is referring to."

"What?" Miki faced him again. "Oh."

Her cheeks flushed a darker shade of red and she tucked

her chin against her chest as she turned away from his stare. It pissed him off that she would want to hide, but at the same time it charmed him. There was no artifice with Miki. What you saw was what you got. Everything about her was natural, the colour of her hair, the make-up-free face, the breasts plumped up in her tank top and the words that came out of her mouth. She was a refreshing change from the women in his recent past. Grant was ashamed to admit his choices hadn't been the most well thought out when it came to women.

Like most young men he'd been after one thing, and until Mikaila stepped back into his life he'd been content. Not any longer. Now he wanted far more than the hollow physical satisfaction he'd limited himself to experiencing. Grant couldn't deny the selections he'd made had decided the outcome before any of his previous relationships had begun. But Miki was different in every way that mattered, which meant he couldn't coast along and enjoy the ride. He had to take control or risk another crash and burn. That wasn't even an option with Miki.

The wind picked up and Grant glanced at the sky to see a storm rolling in from the south. They'd been so occupied with their sandcastle building they hadn't seen the change in weather. The clouds were moving fast and unless they packed up and headed home now they'd be caught in the deluge when it hit.

"Come on, time to head home." He indicated the dark grey mass on the horizon.

"Damn. Looks like a doozy too," Dayne said as his sat back on his haunches.

"I guess the weatherman got it right for a change." Miki pushed to her feet and slapped her hands together to brush off the sand. "They said we'd be getting a thunderstorm in the early evening, but it's been such a lovely day I thought for sure they'd gotten it wrong again."

"It has been a great day, and just because the weather is going to turn foul doesn't mean our fun has to end. How about dinner and a movie, complete with popcorn and choc tops in a private movie theatre?" Grant asked.

"Buttered popcorn?"

"Whatever kind you want," Dayne said.

"Romantic comedy?"

Grant groaned. "If we have to. But fair's fair, next movie we get to pick."

Miki smiled. "I know just the one I want to watch."

"Which one? We've probably got it at the house but if not we can pick it up at the rental store," Grant said as he reached for Miki's hand and pulled her up the beach towards the car.

"*No Strings Attached.*"

"I think that came in yesterday's bundle."

"Yesterday's bundle?"

They stopped at the outdoor shower to hose off their feet. "Yeah, we get online and order new movies all the time. Our latest package came yesterday, but I can't remember what was in it."

"I'm pretty sure I ordered *No Strings Attached.*" Dayne held on to Miki as she lifted one leg under the spray. "I definitely know the latest *Saw* movie was in there."

"I'm not watching that." Miki shuddered in an exaggerated fashion. "Too much blood and guts for me."

"I can think of something you could do to take your mind off the bad scenes." Dayne waggled his eyebrows.

Grant and Miki laughed at him but in usual Dayne style he affected a wounded look and kept going.

"I'm crushed you two don't take me seriously. I was being genuine. I was only going to suggest Miki refill our drinks and the popcorn bowl during the blood and guts parts."

Smiling, Miki said, "Sure you were." Shaking the excess

water from her legs, she stepped back onto the grass. "We're going to get your car filthy and wet if we get in like this."

"There's a couple of towels in the boot. We can use those to dry off before getting in. Not that it matters, I'll put it in for a detail during the week," Grant said.

She frowned at him. "Don't you wash your own car?"

"Well, yeah, but the car wash across the road from the office has this new system and...never mind." Grant draped his arm over her shoulders and pulled her close. "Let's go. What do you want for dinner?"

"We could do homemade pizza. That would make it a real movie date," Dayne said from the other side of Miki.

"You guys make your own pizzas?" She laughed. "I don't think I've ever met a pair of more domesticated men in my life."

"Hey." Dayne bumped her hip with his. "Don't knock us until you've experienced the joys that are my hand-rolled pizza dough."

"Crispiest crust you'll ever eat." Grant let her go and pulled his keys from his pocket. With the press of a button, the doors unlocked and he popped the boot to grab the beach towels stowed in the back. "Here." He flung one at Dayne and turned to Miki with the other.

"Thanks."

Grant stood mesmerized as Miki wrapped the towel around her waist and shimmied out of her shorts. With one tug he could pull that strip of cloth from her and find out what she wore beneath the denim, but he wasn't sure he could control himself if he knew, and screwing her in the car park wasn't exactly the gentlemanly thing to do. He almost swallowed his tongue when she stripped off her tank top and revealed the skimpy bra beneath. Miki shook both pieces of clothing before tossing them into the trunk and getting in the car.

"She's gonna go home like that?" Dayne's strangled words snapped Grant out of his trance.

He closed his eyes and sucked in a deep breath. "If she is I'll be lucky to keep the car on the road." Grant snatched the towel from Dayne and roughly cleaned up before sliding behind the wheel.

His friend slipped in beside him, but neither of them braved a look into the backseat. Grant even tilted the rear-view mirror so he wouldn't see Miki every time he checked traffic. With jerky movements, Grant started the car and put it in reverse. He stopped. Now he'd have to check the mirrors, look over his shoulder. With a groan, he clenched his jaw and swivelled his head so quickly he looked like one of those amusement clowns on speed.

There was no traffic in sight so he took his foot off the break and jammed it on the accelerator. They lurched back and forth with his crappy driving and Dayne's hand slammed onto the dashboard. He thought he caught a glimpse of Miki toppling to the side as he swung the wheel and shoved the car into drive. Again, Grant's driving was less than stellar but he couldn't unclench his jaw to apologise. His only concern was getting them home before the thought of Miki almost naked in his backseat did dangerous things to his control.

Weaving in and out of traffic with total disregard for the speed limit, Grant raced home, his car zooming down the roads like the lust in his veins. Fast. It took twenty minutes to get home. Dayne pressed the garage remote as they drove up the street and Grant swung the Audi in the garage before the door was all the way up. Braking hard, he shifted into park and undid his seatbelt. When he cut the engine the whirr of a motor filled the silence as the door lowered behind them.

"Jeez, Grant. Are the hounds of hell on our tails?" Miki's laughter filled the car and snapped the last of his control.

He looked at Dayne, and without words they both opened their doors and got out. In unison they opened the rear doors and moved in on her. Blood pumped through him in a scalding flash flood. His cock pressed against the confines of his shorts and rubbed against the sensitive head.

"What?" Miki's gaze darted between them.

"If you don't want me driving like a lunatic don't get in my car naked," he growled.

"I'm not naked."

"You soon will be." Dayne grabbed the towel and ripped it away. "Oh man."

"Christ. What the hell are those?" Grant pointed at the tiny web of black covering her pussy.

"What?" Miki looked down. "They're my underwear."

"That's not underwear. That's, that's, hell, I have no idea what that is but it certainly isn't underwear," Grant argued.

"I'll have you know they're very expensive underwear."

"I'll write you a check." Grant stuck his fingers into the lacy webbing and ripped them apart. The sound of tearing cloth was drowned out by Miki's gasp.

"Grant!"

He didn't answer her. Instead he pulled her into his arms and took her protesting mouth with his. She melted into him, her tongue coming out to play with his. Closing his eyes, Grant dove into her lush depths while attempting to rid her of her only other clothing. Dayne's hands pushed his aside and disposed of her bra. Miki moaned and he swallowed the sound before it could escape. Letting go of her lips, he trailed his mouth across her cheek to her ear.

"We're going to fuck you in my car, Miki." He nipped at her lobe and she jolted against him. "You want that don't you?"

The nod of her head wasn't enough. He needed the words.

"Say it." He sucked on her lobe before licking his way back to her mouth. "Tell us to fuck you in the car, Miki."

"Please."

Dayne was playing with her breasts with one hand and plying her clit with the other. She humped against his friend, her legs spread as wide as they could go with them on either side of her. Grant lowered his hand to join Dayne's and together they thrust a finger into her clenching channel.

"Please." The raw cry tore from her throat.

"Say it!"

They worked her flesh, drove in and out while keeping the pressure on her clit. Grant twisted his hand, brought his thumb to her anus and pushed just the tip inside.

"Oh, oh, yes. Yes. Fuck me."

DAYNE SUCKED a nipple into his mouth and she shattered on their hands. Her hips thrashed and bucked as she milked as much pleasure from them as she could.

"Jesus." Dayne pulled away, leaned into the front seat and scrambled for his wallet. He came back with two condoms and neither of them wasted time stripping out of their clothes and donning the protection.

Grant lifted Miki from the seat, her body pliant with her release, and manoeuvred underneath her. Dayne helped turn her to face Grant and lowered her onto his friend's cock. Grant shuddered in reaction as the hot glove of her cunt settled over him. If Dayne was any judge, his friend was close to the edge and things would be over before he got a chance to join in.

"Hurry up," Grant demanded.

"Can't fit. Move your legs along the seat towards me." Dayne helped guide both of them into position.

"Dayne, please," Miki gasped. "I need both of you."

He ran his fingers through the cream coating her pussy and spread it over her arse. He did it again and again, trying to get as much lubrication as possible to ease his entry. Dayne pushed a finger inside her tight passage. A second followed and she rode his hand as she worked herself along the length of Grant's cock.

"Now."

"Dammit, you're not ready."

Miki turned her head to look at him. Her eyes blazed with an icy-blue flame that threatened to incinerate him. "Now, Dayne. Fuck my arse now."

A violent shudder racked his entire body at her words. Removing his fingers, he crawled up behind her. One knee on the seat, the other on the floor, Dayne pressed the head of his erection to her puckered hole. Miki rocked her hips and took him in. She opened for him, relaxing her muscles until the mushroom tip popped through the tight ring. Fire shot up his cock and he slammed forward with a roar.

He stilled, frightened his hasty entry had hurt her, but she bucked beneath him. Her arse sucked at his length as she rode up and down. Dayne couldn't see how it was possible, but she directed their lovemaking, caught between him and Grant, she moved with speed and drove him quickly to the edge of release. Fumbling for purchase, he thrust into her as best he could in the confined space of the backseat. His friend lay pinned under both of them and could do no more than enjoy the ride.

In no time, Dayne felt the spasms in his balls signalling his imminent orgasm. The sight of his cock disappearing between those plump cheeks sent him over. His hips powered back and forth, his length sawing in and out, as he gave in and exploded. Come blasted through his shaft, filling the condom in jet after jet of hot seed. Stars burst in front of his eyes and he squeezed them shut as the last wave stole his breath.

Miki jerked against him, her muscles milking his softening flesh as she came. Dayne wasn't sure who cried what. The moan, the growl, the shout. It didn't matter. With a final plunge, he buried himself deep and fell forward, his sweat-slick chest sliding along her shaking spine. He heard Grant gasp and felt his friend's cock pulse against his own through the thin layer of Miki's body. As he came back to earth the only sounds were the three of them struggling to catch their breath.

He eased out of Miki's arse and sat half on the floor, half on the seat. His legs shook and he didn't trust them to hold him up just yet. Dayne spotted his shirt and used it to wrap the condom in. They should go inside and get cleaned up, but he couldn't find the energy to speak, never mind move.

"I'll never walk again."

Dayne smoothed a hand over Miki's rump. "Yes, you will. And if not I'm happy for you to stay right here forever." He slid his fingers through her slit and brushed her protruding clit. Grant's spent cock, wrapped in the condom lay below her. Dayne marvelled at how the sight didn't worry him. This sharing Miki was teaching him new things about himself every minute they were together.

"I'm not staying here like this," she murmured. "I can only imagine how horrible I must look."

Idly he played with the folds of her pussy. "Miki, honey, you are the fucking sexiest thing I've ever laid eyes on." He thrust two fingers into her well-fucked cunt and she trembled around him.

"Oh..."

He smiled. The woman amazed him. They fucked her senseless and yet still he could arouse her. She rocked onto him, moaning and whimpering as cream flowed from her. His cock pulsed, hardened with renewed interest. They so needed to get inside. Dayne removed his fingers and slapped her arse.

"Come on, lazy bones, time to go inside."

"Hey, that hurt."

"No, it didn't." He patted the slightly pink imprint of his hand. Seeing his mark on her white skin did strange things to his insides. They might have to do some exploring later.

"Dayne's right. We need to move inside." Grant sat, taking Miki with him.

"Damn you both." Her words were said without heat.

"And you right along with us, baby." Dayne got out of the car, his legs remaining solid.

Reaching down, he scooped Miki up into his arms and carried her through the door connecting the garage to the house. He headed straight for Grant's shower. Depositing Miki on her feet, he leaned over and turned on the water. Grant followed them into the bathroom.

"I'll get clean towels and something for Miki to wear."

Dayne left the room as Grant herded her under the hot spray. It took mere seconds to pull sweats and shirts from the clean laundry for him and Miki. Circling around via the linen room, he pulled out an armload of fresh towels and headed back to Grant's room. His friend was stepping out when he got back.

"I'm done." He reached for one of the towels. "Miki's still washing her hair."

Without comment, Dayne put his bundle down on the basin and walked into the shower. He stepped up behind her, pressed his front to her back and wrapped his arms around her. Burying his face in the curve between neck and shoulder, he nuzzled her, drawing a gasp from her throat.

"You always smell so good."

Miki laughed. "Yeah, right. Sweaty and sandy isn't what I'd consider an appealing scent."

"On you anything would be appealing."

He let her go and reached for the soap. Dayne lathered up quickly, washing away the sand and sweat. Miki finished rinsing her hair and edged past him. With eyes only for her while she dried her body and wrapped a towel around her head, he finished up and switched off the water. She handed him a dry towel and he indicated the clothes he'd brought in.

"There's a pair of drawstring shorts and T-shirt for you to wear. We'll put your clothes in the washer before dinner."

"Thanks."

The shorts were miles too big, but she pulled the cord tight and managed to hold them up. His shirt fit better, but only because it was one of the smallest he owned. It would have to do for now. Besides, they'd have her naked again before the night was over.

"Where did Grant disappear to?"

"No idea. Let's go find out." Dayne curled his fingers around hers. "Hopefully he's put a pot of coffee on. I could do with a caffeine boost."

"I wouldn't mind one either. I'm suddenly feeling very sleepy."

"You can have a nap if you want."

"Oh, no. If I sleep now I'll never sleep tonight."

He looked at her and grinned. "That's not such a bad thing."

She playfully punched his arm. "Stop that. Haven't you had enough of me already?"

"Not in this lifetime." He was dead serious, but Miki either didn't get it or chose to ignore his intention.

"So where is your movie collection so I can pick out what to watch?"

The change of subject didn't worry him too much. The topic did mean she was sticking around for the evening and that was a bonus as far as Dayne was concerned. "Let's see what Grant's up to first, then I'll show you what we've got."

"Okay, but I'm still not watching anything with blood and guts."

Dayne sigh and tried to add disappointment to his voice. "All right."

Miki giggled. "That was shocking. Good thing you didn't go into acting or you would have starved to death by now."

He smiled at her. "Yeah, owning C.S. is a hell of a lot more fun anyway."

"You never did tell me what C.S. stands for."

"Cool Shit," Grant came out of the laundry. "Our clothes are in the washer."

"What?" Miki gawked at them. "You named your business Cool Shit?"

Laughing at the disbelief in her voice Dayne said, "No, we called it C.S. No one but Grant and I know what the letters stand for."

"And now that we've told you you're sworn to secrecy or we'll have to kill you." Grant's dead-pan face made Dayne laugh harder.

"Kill me how?" The smirk on her lips told him she enjoyed playing along.

"Well." Grant rubbed his hand over his chin. "I was thinking we could start by seeing if we could kill you with orgasms, and if that didn't work I seem to recall someone being very ticklish."

They lunged for her together.

6

MIKI SQUEALED and tore off down the hallway towards the lounge room. Dayne caught her by the arm and Grant quickly took advantage and grabbed her legs. Lifting her up, they walked over to the couch and sat, side by side, with her spread across their laps.

"So, what will it be? Death by tickling?" Grant's long fingers wrapped around her ankle to hold her foot still while he attacked the sole of her foot with his other hand. She kicked but his forearm pinned her legs to his.

"No. Don't. Stop." Her words blurting out between panted breaths. Dayne's arms banded around her middle and his fingers dug into each side of her ribs, sending her into peals of laughter. They each tortured whatever part of her they held until she gasped for breath.

"Or..." Dayne push one hand up the baggy leg of her shorts. "Death by orgasm?"

"Oh God."

His fingers brushed her folds, searched out her clit and stopped.

"Don't..."

"Tickle?" Grant renewed his assault on her feet.

"Or orgasm?" Dayne applied pressure to the tender bundle of nerves under his thumb and the move sent a jolt of pleasure into her core. "God, you're so wet."

A breathless cry followed the fingers he'd thrust inside her slippery pussy. "Orgasm!"

He probed deeper. "Does being chased down turn you on, Miki?"

"Oh."

"Jesus. Your muscles just squeezed the fuck out of my fingers." He pulled out, pushed in. "Would you like it if we tied you down? If we caught you to keep? To do with as we pleased?" His fingers curled, found her G-spot and sent spasms through her core. "You're so fucking hot."

She squirmed on their laps but he didn't let up, and when Grant's hand joined Dayne's, Miki knew she would be seeing stars before they were done. If they kept this up she surely would die. Her pussy was still swollen and sensitive from their sex in the car. The pleasure so intense it bordered on pain. In seconds, she was screaming over the edge and coming hard. Panting for breath, she slumped, splayed across their legs.

"Christ, your responsiveness blows me away." Grant removed his fingers from her body and brought them to his lips. "And you smell and taste divine."

Miki watched from under lowered lids as he proceeded to lick his wet fingers clean. Her pussy clenched, his obvious enjoyment tightening her lower belly.

Dayne wiggled the fingers still buried in her core and a second less powerful orgasm rocked her. Her back arched as the wave of release broke over her. He gentled his strokes, eased her down until the buzz of pleasure hummed in her veins. Miki closed her eyes and let herself drift with the contentment their magical touch made her feel.

Cradled against Dayne's chest with Grant massaging her calf muscles, Miki could easily believe she'd died and gone to heaven. In fact she'd be quite happy for them to kill her again and again. Just not yet, but definitely later.

"I checked the DVD's while you were in the shower. We have *No Strings Attached*."

"You do? Good."

A clap of thunder shook the house and Miki's eyes popped open. The room had darkened considerably and a flash of lightning was followed seconds later by another boom that made her jump. They turned to look out the windows. The sky was black and the trees were swaying violently in the wind which was picking up by the minute. Rain started in an avalanche. There was no sprinkle to downpour, just a deluge like a dam had burst.

"That's one angry storm."

"Good thing we made it home before it started," Grant said.

"I think it's our cue to get dinner happening." Dayne stood, taking Miki with him.

"Hey."

"Shush. What do you want on your pizza?"

"Do you have pepperoni?"

"Of course. What decent pizza parlour wouldn't?" Dayne set her on her feet. "You can help Grant get the toppings ready while I make the dough."

Miki followed Dayne into the kitchen and waited for them to tell her what to do. All three of them bumped shoulders as they washed their hands and playfully fought over the handtowel.

"Here." Grant pulled out a stool at the island bench. "Sit here and I'll get you a chopping board and knife."

She studied them as they pulled ingredients from the fridge and pantry. Dayne cleared the counter next to the sink and took bowls, measuring cups and spoons from cupboards and drawers. He worked quickly, turning flour, water, salt and some other spices she couldn't see the name of into a ball of dough.

"How long does that have to rise?" she asked.

"It doesn't." He smiled at her over his shoulder. "That's the secret to my perfect thin crust."

"Oh, I would never have thought to make a base like that."

"Here. Don't slice the pepperoni too thin." Grant laid a long roll of processed meat on the board in front of her.

"Not a problem. I prefer it on the thick side too. Do you want the whole knob sliced?"

"Yeah, between the three of us we'll need it." Grant pulled out a food processor and started grating the three cheeses he'd pulled from the refrigerator.

"What's with the different cheeses?"

"That's another secret to the perfect pizza," Grant said.

"It took years of experimenting to come up with the right combination," Dayne added.

"Isn't mozzarella the perfect pizza cheese?" She glanced between them.

Dayne turned to face her, his expression serious. "It is. But there is so much more to be added, and we would not be true pizza connoisseurs without searching out the right combination of taste, texture and smell." He bowed low. "It's our duty to discover the best."

"I'm humbled by your sacrifice. It surely must have been a trial to eat all those pizzas." She couldn't stop the giggle breaking free. Dayne's shenanigans got sillier the more time they spent together. But Miki wasn't really surprised. He'd always been the one to make her laugh in high school. And him paired with Grant only made sure the good times were doubled.

"Do you mock us, woman?" Dayne took a step towards her.

"No, no, really. I appreciate all you've suffered." Grinning, she ducked her head and got back to cutting the pepperoni.

"You'll keep." Miki peeked at Dayne through lowered lashes. "And when you least expect it..."

If it was anything like the last time they'd come after her, Miki was sure any punishment they dished out wouldn't be too hard to take. She finished slicing the meat and curiosity got the better of her, she slipped off her seat and headed over to where Grant was mixing the grated cheeses in a large bowl.

"Are you going to tell me what types of cheese you use?"

"You've already guessed one." His fingers worked through the shreds of yellow, tossing and mixing them together. "Mozzarella, tasty and parmesan. In equal portions."

"I don't think I've ever had pizza with anything but mozzarella before." She tried to sneak some cheese but he slapped her fingers away.

"Then you're in for a treat. In fact, I'd bet money you won't have tried anything better." Grant smiled at her and Miki leaned up and kissed his cheek. "What was that for?"

She shrugged. "Just because." Miki couldn't even tell herself what had prompted the impulse.

"Hey, bring that 'just because' on over here," Dayne called.

Smiling, Miki walked over and planted a kiss on Dayne's bristly jaw. "Need help with anything else?"

"Sure, turn the oven on hot. I'll grab the stone out in a second and you can put that in to heat."

"Stone?"

"It's a ceramic tile that you heat and cook your pizza on. It imitates a pizza oven," Dayne explained.

"Oh, you mean like the wood-fire ones where the pizza is slid onto the bottom of the oven?"

"Yep."

"Wow. I can't wait to try this. I love wood-fire pizza."

Dayne grabbed her chin with his hand. "Well, you're going to be in love with me and my pizza before the night is out." He pressed his lips to hers, in a hard smacking kiss.

She was sure his words were meant as a joke, but her stupid heart flipped in her chest and butterflies swarmed in her stomach. Miki didn't want to fall for either of them, but it was hard not to. Both men appealed to her for different reasons as well as the same reasons. The boys she remembered with fondness had grown into men worth knowing. They were men who took life seriously while still being able to have fun, unlike her husband who'd never taken anything serious in his short life. In some ways David had reminded her of Dayne and Grant, which, Miki was ashamed to say, was probably part of the reason she'd been drawn to him in the first place.

Dayne studied her, stared into her eyes as though he could read her mind, and Miki quickly shut down her thoughts. When he finally let her go he gave her a pat on the arse.

"Go turn the oven on high."

Miki walked on unsteady legs. Her insides a swirling mass of emotion she didn't know how to untangle. She needed to talk to Frankie. It was strange of Frankie to not call her. At home earlier today, she'd rung her friend's home and mobile numbers. Left messages on both voicemails for her to ring Grant's number, but she still hadn't heard from her. Miki cursed herself for leaving her phone in Frankie's car last night.

"Grant, Frankie hasn't rung has she?"

"No, but my phone is in the bedroom. We might not have heard it ring over the storm."

"Can I go check?"

"Of course you can." Grant's brow creased. "I told you there was no need to ask me for my phone."

"I know but..." She shrugged. "I feel funny not asking."

He frowned at her. "Go get the phone and if she hasn't rung give her a call. We've got dinner under control."

"Okay. Thanks."

Miki strode down the hall. She couldn't tell if the anxiety churning in her stomach was because she hadn't heard from Frankie or because of the situation with Dayne and Grant. Either way, a few minutes conversation with her best friend would help right about now.

GRANT TURNED ON DAYNE. "What the hell are you doing?"

"What?" Dayne's ignorance just pissed him off more.

"Are you *trying* to scare her out the door?"

"What the fuck are you talking about?"

"That 'going to love me' bullshit."

The puzzled expression on his friend's face managed to pull his anger back a notch. Did Dayne really have no clue about Miki's reaction? "She froze up when you said that."

"I didn't mean it the way it sounded. Well, I did, but it wasn't intentional. It just slipped out while we were mucking around." Dayne shook his head. "I can't censor my words or my feelings because Miki might freak out. It's not natural and you know it."

With a sigh, Grant leaned on the counter. "I know. I just don't want to fuck it up, man."

"And we won't." Dayne crossed his arms over his chest. "As much as I want to let the cards fall wherever, I can't. If I'm not already in love with her I'm well on the way and I want to share that with her. I'm not asking for her to return my feelings, but I want Miki to know how I feel about her."

"Yeah, I get that." He scrubbed a hand down his face. "But I still think you need to back the truck up a bit. Things are moving fast and they could easily spiral out of control if we're not careful."

"Dammit, Grant. You know I'm not one to hold back what I'm thinking or feeling."

"Maybe just try to curb it a little for now?"

A muscle in the side of Dayne's jaw twitched. For long seconds his friend didn't say anything, and Grant thought they were about to have one of their rare fights. He held his breath, waiting for the explosion, but when it came it wasn't what he'd expected.

"Fine." Dayne threw his hands in the air and stalked off to the pantry. "I'll keep my mouth shut from now on."

"That's not what I mean and you know it." Grant followed him across the room. "Come on, Dayne, we can't screw this up."

The desperation in his voice pulled him up short. *Whoa. Okay, so this was new.* He'd never felt this clawing, urgent lash for anything—anyone—until now. No wonder he was striking out at Dayne. Like a cornered feral animal, he was swiping at the nearest thing. Grant prided himself on his control and right now he was as far from the steering wheel as he could get. Hell, he wasn't even on the bus. Miki held the power. The question was whether she'd pull over and let them on or run them over at warp speed.

Dayne came out of the pantry and crashed into him. "Sorry."

"No. I'm sorry. I took my frustration out on you and I shouldn't have."

His friend shrugged. "No biggie. We're both tense at the moment."

"I feel like I've been put through the wringer and we haven't even scratched the surface yet."

"Look, let's not borrow trouble ahead of time. Like you said earlier today, one step at a time."

Grant knew his own advice made sense, but that was before he'd found himself in deeper than he'd ever imagined being. It was easy to spout wisdom when you weren't caught in the whirlwind of emotions of falling in love. He'd never dreamed it would happen this fast. He always pictured love to be slow, sure, comfortable. The emotions he was experiencing were fast, uncertain and so restrictive it was like having a ten tonne truck parked on his chest.

"Come on, let's get these pizzas made and in the oven." Dayne thumped him on the back as he walked past.

He tried to lasso in his emotions and make some logical thought patterns. Nothing would come together, but he didn't have time to brood. Miki entered the kitchen with his phone to her ear. Her brow was creased and she'd caught her bottom lip between her teeth. The curve looked red and puffy from chewing and Grant walked over to remove that lush flesh from any further damage. With the tip of his finger, he tapped her mouth.

"Stop that. You'll make your lip bleed if you're not careful."

She let go of her lip and mouthed sorry as she put her hand up in a stop signal.

"You still haven't returned my calls. Where are you, Frankie? I'm starting to worry. Ring me on this number because you've got my phone. Bye."

"Still can't reach her?"

"No, and it's not like her. I'm worried."

"I wouldn't be." If what Grant suspected was true, Miki might not get hold of Frankie for a while yet.

"What aren't you telling me?"

He glanced at Dayne for help, but his friend held up his hands and took a step back. "You started this."

"What? Started what?" Miki's voice held a note of panic.

"Relax. I'm sure she's fine." Grant waited until her gaze locked with his. "She's probably just hung over or something."

"Or something." Dayne's comment drew Miki's gaze again.

"What are you two talking about? Did something happen to Frankie at the party last night?"

"No, no. Nothing like that." Grant threw a dirty look Dayne's way. "I, well, it's just..."

"What, what? It's just what?" Her gaze swivelled between them.

Grant gripped Miki's shoulders. "Stop it, there's nothing to worry about. Frankie is fine as far as we know, it's just that I don't think she went home alone, that's all."

"What?" She stared at him as her knees buckled and she sat on the edge of a stool. "No way? Frankie picked someone up?"

Grant nodded as he took the chair next to her.

"She certainly did," Dayne added.

Miki's attention was drawn back to Dayne and Grant knew the grin on his friend's face said they hadn't revealed everything.

Her eyes narrowed. "Spill. Who'd she pick up?"

Dayne laughed. "You won't believe us if we tell you."

"Sure I will, why would either of you lie?"

"She left with Alec Harris," Grant said.

"*Alley Cat?* Bullshit." Miki jerked her head around and stared at him with her mouth open.

"Nope, no bull. As you said, why would we lie?" Dayne added.

"Hell. He's the last guy Frankie would hook up with. She used to carry on about hating him, despising him, but every time she looked at him, well, I've never seen her look at anyone else that way."

"Maybe it's a case of protesting too much? Besides, we're not in school anymore, Miki." Grant asked.

"Maybe." Miki chewed on her lip again as she sat in stunned silence. He could almost hear the gears in her mind turning.

"She'll ring when she gets your messages. In the meantime, how about we go get the movie ready while Dayne finishes off the pizzas and puts them in the oven?" Grant got to his feet and pulled her with him.

"You said you had *No Strings Attached*, right?"

He laid his arm over her shoulders and hugged her close as he walked towards the media room. "Yep, we do. But we've got some others you might want to watch instead."

"I'm not watching *Saw*."

Grant laughed. "Don't worry, we're not watching that one. Don't tell Dayne, but I'm with you when it comes to that franchise, way too much blood and guts for my liking."

"Really? I thought all guys went for that type of thing."

"I'm not against it in general, but those films just take it too far."

"So what type of movie do you normally watch?"

"I don't have one genre I prefer over another. As long as it's entertaining I really don't care."

"So you're good with watching this one?" Miki held up a DVD case.

"Miki, it's about a guy who hooks up with his best *girl* friend for no-strings sex, what's not to like?"

"Well, when you say it like that it's got to be every guy's

fantasy movie." She laughed as she took the disk out. "So where's the player?"

Grant pushed on the wall panel next to the screen. "Here."

"Holy shit." Miki peered into the opening. "This is like mission control."

"We've got the equipment to play any form of media in this little cupboard."

"Is that a game console?"

"Yeah, we've got them all in here."

"You play games on that screen?" Miki turned to stare at the wall on their right.

"It is a little excessive, but it's a tax write-off, so why not?"

"A tax write-off?"

"We have to test the stock that we sell at C.S. somewhere." He grinned. This was definitely one perk of owning a business he loved.

"So what else does C.S. stock? Other than big boys' toys?"

"We have a range of gadgets for women and kids as well, but our big sellers are the men's items." He took the disk from her and popped it into the DVD player. "Okay, now we're ready whenever dinner is."

"Do you have a computer around here somewhere? I'd like to check my emails if I can."

"Sure, there's one in the office." Grant entwined their fingers and pulled her out of the room. Passing Dayne in the kitchen, he said, "How long?"

"Fifteen minutes."

"Okay, Miki wants to check her email while we wait." He led her across the lounge room and into the home office they'd set up.

"Wow." She stopped just inside the door. "You guys really do have all the latest technology don't you?"

"Perks of the job." He walked around his desk and jiggled

his mouse. "Here, you can use my PC." Grant indicated she sit in his chair.

"Thanks. It'll only take me a few minutes. I just have to check how today went."

"Today?"

She was tapping away at the keyboard. "Um, yeah, I help Frankie with Playgrounds for Hope. There was a gala day on out at Penrith. Barbara was going to email me the details." Distracted, she didn't even look at him as she clicked through screens. "Oh boy. Frankie is gonna love those numbers."

"What numbers?" It fascinated him, witnessing her joy as she read through her mail.

"Uh."

He smiled. She was kinda cute preoccupied. "What numbers, Miki?"

"Oh, right." She tapped madly at the keyboard again. "Give me a sec." The corners of her eyes crinkled and a smile stretched her lips as she answered Barbara. Finally, with a click of the mouse she sat back and looked at him. "There. All done."

"So I take it the day went well?"

"Oh, yeah. It went brilliantly. We got another major bene-factor out of it too. Frankie will be pleased."

"You keep saying that. What does it have to do with Frankie?"

"She's Playgrounds for Hope. It's a charity for underprivi-leged kids. We've been up and running for ten years now. Getting bigger and better every year too."

"We? You're part of it?"

"I donate time and my management skills to the organisa-tion. Plus the occasional hands-on day. But that doesn't happen very often because we've got a great group of volunteers who handle that end of it."

She kept surprising him. Grant never would have guessed

she'd be involved in something that huge. And he knew it was big because he knew what Playgrounds for Hope was, knew all about the wonderful things they did for kids below the poverty line. C.S. had even employed a couple of teenagers last year in one of the charity's many drives to better the underprivileged's lives. He and Dayne had already talked about hiring on more of the kids when they did the employment drive again this year and this new piece of information sealed the deal as far as he was concerned.

"Dinner," Dayne yelled from the other end of the house. Grant rolled his eyes. It wouldn't even occur to Dayne to walk over here and tell them.

MIKI CUDDLED into Dayne's side. She'd been asleep for about twenty minutes and he didn't have the heart to wake her. They'd watched three movies, well two and a half. She hadn't quite made the last one. Her legs were draped over Grant's lap and his friend was idly rubbing her feet. Dayne reached for the remote and nearly toppled the bowl of leftover popcorn. Trying not to disturb Miki, he managed to save the popcorn and grab the remote. Angling the device at the far wall, he pressed a button and stopped the movie.

"We don't want to watch the rest do we?"

Grant yawned. "No. I think it's bedtime."

"Yours?"

"There's more room."

"Carry or wake?"

"May as well go with what we've got."

"Works for me."

"Let me get up." Grant lifted Miki's legs and slid out from under her. "Okay, how do you want to do this?"

"I can carry her if you help me off the lounge, or you can take her and I'll switch everything off and lock up." Miki stirred and snuggled in closer.

"I'll lock up. She looks too comfy to disturb." With his hands on her waist, Grant took enough of Miki's weight for Dayne to scoot forward and get an arm under her legs. Turning her into his chest, he pushed to his feet with Grant steadying them both. "Got her?"

"Yeah." Dayne stepped across the room with a sleeping Miki.

"I'll be in as soon as I've switched off and locked up." Grant followed behind, flicking the switch to cut the power to the media room as he went.

He walked down the dim hallway and into Grant's room. Moonlight flooded through the windows, illuminating the area so lights weren't necessary. Beyond the open shutters Dayne could see the star-filled sky. One thing he loved about summer storms was the gorgeous just-washed look they gave the sky once they moved on. The bed dominated the room. Until this weekend with Miki he'd thought Grant's huge handmade bed frame a waste of space. Now he could fully appreciate the large-size mattress.

Laying her gently on the bed, Dayne reached over to pull back one side of the covers. He was about to move her over when Grant came in.

"Should get her out of those clothes, she'll be more comfortable without them on." His friend stripped off his shirt as he headed for the bathroom.

"I'm getting there," Dayne whispered so he didn't wake her.

Slipping the sweats down her legs was easy once he pulled the drawstring loose. The shirt was another matter. He'd have to get it over her arms and head, and for the life of him he couldn't see how it was possible without waking Miki up.

Dayne was still pondering the dilemma when Grant came to bed.

"What are you waiting for?"

Dayne stared at his friend. What the hell was he waiting for? "I didn't want to wake her." His explanation sounded stupid to his own ears, he could only imagine what Grant thought.

"If we do it quickly she won't wake. Or at least not enough to stay awake," Grant said as he climbed on the opposite side of the bed.

Stripping out of his clothes, Dayne kneeled on the edge of the mattress and reached for the hem of Miki's shirt. "You lift her up, I'll take it off."

Grant slid his hands under her top and picked her up. Dayne raised the shirt past her stomach and chest but it got tangled up around her shoulders as he tried to pull her arms free.

"Hey." Her sleepy voice held confusion.

"You need to get undressed. It's bedtime," Dayne said.

"Did the movie finish already?"

Grant chuckled. "Yes, Miki, the movie finished."

"Can we watch another one?"

"Miki, it's after midnight. Time for sleep." Dayne managed to untangle her arms and slip the shirt over her head.

"Okay."

Miki curled on her side and laid her head on the pillow. He thought she'd gone to sleep again but then her eyelids fluttered open and she gazed at him. Dayne wasn't sure what was going through her mind and didn't think he'd be happy if he knew. Confusion and sadness swirled in the bottomless blue of her eyes.

"I wasn't going to stay another night."

His chest constricted. "No?"

She shook her head. "It's far too easy to stay."

"There's nothing easy about you being here," Dayne whispered.

Her eyes full of resignation, she murmured, "I know."

"We'll make it work, Miki." Grant leaned against the headboard.

"How?" She turned to look over her shoulder. "How does anyone make something like this work, Grant? Thinking we can have any more than this one weekend is foolish and stupid. Someone is bound to get hurt if not all of us. I can't pretend this could be something it can't. I'll never do that again."

Dayne caressed her cheek with a fingertip. "Why not just live in the moment? Enjoy what we have and worry about the rest when it comes. You can't deny you want to be here, Miki."

"I'm not." She leaned her face into his palm, rubbed against him like a cat. "There's no doubt for any of us that I want to be here, with both of you, but this isn't the real world. We've wrapped ourselves in a bubble and the minute we step outside the whole thing will burst."

He hated the pain on her face, in her eyes, but he couldn't think of any words that would make it go away. The ones he wanted to utter would only send her running, and she was close to doing that now.

"We stepped outside today, Miki, and nothing came crashing down."

Grant's words were true, they had ventured out as a three-some. Sure, they hadn't really pushed any social boundaries, but they'd made a start.

Dayne stretched out next to Miki and propped his head on one hand while stroking her arm with the other. The silkiness of her skin intrigued him—the covering of fine hair, the sprinkle of freckles in a multitude of browns and reds on a backdrop of milky white. Dayne could spend forever exploring every inch of her.

"Do you really think we can take today as the norm?" Miki asked.

"No, but then even in the most normal circumstances not every day is a picnic." Dayne argued.

Miki yawned, her hand coming up to cover her mouth.

"Let's not talk about it now. You're tired and things never look good when you're wrung out." He dropped a kiss on her forehead. "Come on, curl up and go to sleep. We'll talk in the morning."

She wiggled over until she was snuggled up against his chest. Dayne wrapped one arm around her waist and the other one under the pillow they shared. Grant slid down and spooned himself to Miki's back. He didn't mind that his hand touched Grant's stomach or that Grant's hand lay on Dayne's waist. It felt right for the three of them to be connected in such a way. Miki's soft breath ruffled the hair on his chest, tickled his nipple and heated his blood, sending arousal through his veins.

His body may want her, but Dayne knew none of them needed another hot and heavy session right now. If they had any hope of taking things to the next level they had to push aside the physical and focus on the emotional. They knew they worked well together in bed, too well to some extent, and it was overshadowing the rest of what they had. From now on he'd concentrate on wooing her heart. He knew they already had her body.

7

GRANT WOKE as the sun peaked over the horizon and shone in through the windows. He should get up and close the shutters before the light got too bright and disturbed Miki or Dayne. But pulling himself away from the warm bundle of woman next to him didn't appeal at all. Her scent surrounded him, filled his room until all he could think about was rolling on top of her and sinking deep inside her warm body. She lay sprawled on her back, naked except for the two arms draped across her stomach. It should be strange to have his best friend asleep on the other side of her, but the only thing he felt at the moment was contentment.

The room grew lighter and he knew it was time to force himself to move or risk Miki waking and leaving. Last night, before they'd gone to sleep, she'd questioned what was happening between them, and with the rising of the sun those concerns would be back. Grant would do anything to put off the conversation that might result in her walking away. With a sigh, he rolled over and sat up. He pushed off the bed and took a step when Miki's voice stopped him.

"Where are you going?"

The sleepy rumble vibrated in his ears and rolled through him with a shudder. He closed his eyes, savouring the sound of Miki first thing in the morning. He turned to take in the sight of her in his bed—eyes closed, one arm flung above her head and the other draped across her breasts.

"Closing the shutters before the sun really comes up."

"It's morning?" Her nose and eyes crinkled up.

"No. Pretend you never saw the light," Dayne grumbled from the other side of the bed.

"Easy to do. I haven't opened my eyes yet." She stretched both arms over her head and arched her back off the bed. "Oh God, I hurt all over. What the hell did we do...?"

Grant watched Miki flush from her toes to her head, the blush turning her freckled complexion a delicate crimson. He forgot all about the shutters. In a second, Grant found himself back on the bed, hands either side of her head with his lips slanting over hers. Nothing mattered except tasting her, taking her. His tongue dipped deep, stroked across her teeth to slide over the smooth flesh beyond. She moaned and the sound caught in their mouths as the kiss went on and on.

The bed beside them sank as Dayne moved closer. Grant felt his friends' hair brush his chest as Dayne sought Miki's breasts with his mouth. Pulling his lips from hers, Grant licked and nipped his way over her chin and down the smooth column of her throat. At the bottom of that sleek line he sucked on the shallow indent where her pulse beat at a frantic pace, before tracing the tip of his tongue along her collarbone. She gasped and arched beneath him when he sank his teeth into her shoulder. Lapping at his mark, Grant soothed the small pain and continued on lower.

Dayne moved higher, took his turn at her mouth, and Grant made a bee-line for the sweet nipple standing at attention. The hard bud stabbed into his tongue and he sucked it to the roof of his mouth, pressing and suckling for long drawn-out minutes. He feasted, licked and nibbled the supple mound of her breast, only to return time and again to that tortured peak. Miki made erotic little noises as she squirmed beneath him. Grant groaned around her flesh, her skin vibrating under his lips.

"Oh, God. Do that again," Miki pleaded breathlessly.

Whether it was a cry for him or Dayne to repeat their actions, Grant didn't know and didn't care. He had plans to explore more of her. Each rib drew his lips, his tongue, his teeth. Grant glanced up to watch her face as he traced the dip of her bellybutton. Dayne leaned in to catch her soft cry when Grant nipped at her hipbone. Caught by the perfect slope between body and thigh, he nuzzled and kissed his way south.

The scent of her arousal surrounded him and her pussy sparkled with the evidence of her pleasure. Grant nudged her legs apart and slid his fingers through the soaked folds of her slit. She bucked into his hand and ground her cunt on his probing digits. Covered with her wet heat, he pushed her towards release. He stroked in and out, two fingers, three.

"Please." Miki writhed on the bed, her hips undulating against his touch.

"Please what, Miki?" Dayne rose to his knees beside her. "What do you want?"

"More. Please, Dayne. Grant. More," she panted.

Dayne reached over, grabbed a condom from the bedside table and he threw it at Grant before leaning back to retrieve another one. Grant pulled his fingers from her clenching channel and quickly sheathed his pulsing cock. Miki wrapped her legs around his hips and, pressing her feet into his arse, she dragged him closer. His latex-covered length slid in her thick cream, back and forth, as he teased them both. Then, with a growl, Grant lined himself up and drove into her.

Both of them moaned as her muscles clung to his invading shaft. Balls deep, he held still, riveted by the feel of her wet heat surrounding him. She bucked off the bed, forcing his length deeper. Control snapped. He retreated, advanced, retreated. The slick glide of rippling walls set a fire in his groin. Miki met him thrust for thrust—both taking and giving in equal measure. Grant ground his pelvis into hers, pressed his weight down and drove her into the mattress.

He glanced up, saw Dayne guiding Miki's mouth to his cock and Grant shuddered at the sight. She went willingly, her tongue darting out to swipe at the plump head before her damp lips parted around his friend's girth and sucked him in.

Dayne threw his head back and groaned. "God, yes. You feel so good."

Grant timed his thrusts with Dayne's and watched his friend fuck her mouth. They set an insistent rhythm and continued to plunge into her body with increasing speed.

"Flick the head with your tongue." Dayne's hands were tangled in Miki's hair. "Oh yeah."

Miki moaned around Dayne's cock. Her head bobbed up and down on the pillow and her hips bucked off the bed, meeting them both with equal demand.

His balls ached and his sac tightened, tucked close to his body. Straining, Grant concentrated on holding off his orgasm until Miki reached hers. He squeezed a hand between them, found her clit and stroked the hard knot. Her body jerked and she lost her suction on Dayne's cock as she cried out with her release. The walls of her cunt clamped around him, seized his shaft before fluttering wildly along the entire length. He drove on, pounding into her as he lost sight and came with a roar in his ears.

Grant collapsed forward, buried in her pulsing channel, his testicles emptied out. Surge after surge of sperm filled the condom. Miki gasped for air beneath him, and with the last of his energy, he pulled free and rolled aside.

DAYNE ROLLED the protection down his length, his hands shaking. He leapt from the bed, grabbed Miki's ankles and flipped her over as he hauled her to the edge. Raising her hips, Dayne brought her to her knees and stepped into her waiting warmth. The first brush of his cock on her wet folds sent a lightning bolt up his spine. Sweat coated his back and chest, trickled down his face. She made him hotter than a furnace in hell, but he embraced the burn. Nothing felt better than the fire that exploded to life whenever he touched her.

She moaned, her back arched and her shoulders dropped to the bed, her face pressed into the sheet. The round curve of her arse surged towards him, her slick pussy sucking at his erection, the crown sinking inside her tight channel. With a groan, he flexed his hips and drove his cock into her clenching depths. Scorched from root to tip, he let the blaze capture him.

Already on the edge from the attention of Miki's mouth, Dayne clung to the rim as he slammed into her. Two thrusts, three. Four, five. He ground his teeth, bit his tongue, but nothing could mask the sheer pleasure of fucking Miki. With embarrassing speed, he toppled over, racked by shudders, his vision blurred along with his mind. Slumping forward, he curled an arm around her waist and searched for that spot that would have her joining him in bliss.

Dayne stroked her clit in the same rhythm as his cock stroked in and out of her cunt. Her muscles contracted, clamping and releasing his length in a wave of pure insanity. Miki came and every nerve ending exploded with the final burst of come squeezed from his balls as she convulsed around him. He was rocked by the intensity and his hips jerked uncontrollably, his breath caught and his knees buckled. They collapsed onto the mattress, both trembling with the final spasms of release and gasping for air.

Still buried in her pussy, his cock jerked as the blood drained away and he slipped free of her hold. Dayne pushed up on his arms, muscles shaking, and lifted the bulk of his weight off her. He stepped back on unsteady legs and fell to the bed beside her.

"Jesus."

"Mmm." Dayne couldn't even form a word. That had to be the single most mind-blowing sex he'd ever had, and they'd done plenty of mind blowing this past weekend.

"Fuck, that was hot to watch," Grant growled from somewhere above him.

"Hope you got a good look because there won't be a repeat performance." Dayne's gut cramped at Miki's words.

"Why the hell not?" Grant's tone was fraught with anxiety.

"I think I'm dead," Miki gasped. "Can't have sex if I'm dead."

Thank God. For a second Dayne thought she meant it was over. It couldn't be over. The sex was getting hotter every time, and his suspicion of how he felt about Miki was now fact. He *was* in love with her. There was no mistaking what he suddenly knew to the very marrow of his bones.

He rolled over, tugged Miki into his arms and cuddled her close. They lay crossways on the bed and Grant scooted around to join them. Spooning along her back, his best friend slung his arm over both of them, his hand planted firmly in the middle of Dayne's back. His heart pinched. This is what he wanted every day for the rest of his life, and he'd be fucked if he let anything or anyone get in the way of them being together.

"God, I love you, Miki."

The words were out before he could stop them. She stiffened between them.

"No." Her whispered word carried all the fear he knew she held inside and some that he had no clue about.

"Yes." He kissed her forehead. "It's the way I feel. I'm not asking for you to reciprocate, well, not yet anyway. All I want is for you to know this isn't just sex for me, not that it ever was." She tried to tug from their embrace.

"Miki. Just hear me out, okay?" Dayne held her tighter. "All I want is a chance to see if we can make this work."

"We can't."

"Why not?" Grant asked.

"Because!"

"That's not an answer." Dayne could feel his anger at her refusal to even listen growing. "We promised not to hold anything back and this is part of it. I love you like I never thought myself possible of and I'm not about to hide it under the bed until you're ready to deal with it. I *need* to work this out, Miki." He didn't like the pleading note in his voice, but he'd get down on his knees and beg if he had to.

"I can't." She wriggled and jerked from their hold and scurried from the bed. "I won't. I did the whole relationship thing once, I can't do it again. Never again."

Her head swivelled from side to side, her gaze scanning the room. She folded her arms around her stomach and clutched at her sides, her fingers digging in to her skin. She stood there, naked, and shivered from head to toe. They weren't going to work through whatever the hell she was scared of quickly. Dayne had the sick feeling they'd be lucky to find out what held her back. She was closing herself off. He could see it in her body language and in her eyes. Those blue orbs held so much fear, so much pain.

"Miki—"

"No. Don't. I need to go." She spun in a circle. "Where are my clothes? Why can't I find my clothes?"

Dayne could hear her panic escalating. They needed to calm her down before she went to pieces completely. It terrified him seeing her like this. The frightened woman in front of them wasn't the Miki they'd come to know.

"I'll get your clothes. They're in the drier." Grant slid off the bed. "Calm down, Miki. We'll all get dressed and talk."

"Talk?" Her brow creased as she looked at Grant. "No, no. I have to go home. I *need* to go home."

Things were going nowhere fast. Dayne jumped to his feet and reached for Miki. She tried to avoid him but he gripped her shoulders and gave her a gentle shake.

"Stop, Miki."

She looked at him with tear-filled eyes and all the wind went out of his sails.

"Oh, baby." He pulled her close, tucked her head under his chin. "Grant's getting your clothes. You can get dressed, okay?"

Grant dashed from the room and Dayne held a shivering Miki against him. There weren't any tears liked he'd expected, but then everything about Miki was unexpected. From the second they'd met all those years ago until now, nothing about their friendship was predictable.

She sighed and warm air blew across his chest. The deep breath seemed to settle her, the shaking stopped and she softened in his arms. Dayne relaxed—his hold on her loosening. Grant returned with her clothes neatly folded and placed them on the bed. Dayne unwound his arms and took a step back.

"Your clothes are on the bed." He looked at Grant. "We'll wait for you in the lounge, okay?"

Dayne waited for Miki to say something but she only nodded, reached past him to collect her clothes and walked to the bathroom. He watched her go and knew it wouldn't be the first time today he saw her walking away.

MIKI'S FINGERS trembled as she fastened her seatbelt, the click echoing in the silent confines of the car. She'd persuaded them to take her home but only after she'd threatened to walk if they didn't. No one spoke as Dayne started the engine and soft music came through the speakers. But Miki wasn't listening. Instead she stared out the side window and saw nothing.

Her emotions were in turmoil. She ran the gamut from joy to terror, from calm to panic and every step in between. Miki knew she wasn't being fair shutting them out in an attempt to gain control. Would she ever master the feelings swamping her? At the moment she didn't think so. Everything was too raw with razor-sharp edges that sliced her to ribbons. Sighing, she leaned back against the leather seat and watched the world whizz by in a blur.

Numb from the onslaught of her agitated senses, Miki didn't notice the people out enjoying the beautiful day. It wasn't until they passed the group of shops down the road from her house that she snapped out of it and sat up straight. They'd arrive in a minute and she wanted to get out of the car and inside as quickly as possible. When Dayne pulled the car into her driveway he didn't switch off the engine and Grant turned to look at her.

"You house is for sale?"

"Yes. It's too big for just me." She wouldn't bore them with the details of the woman suing her for what David had done. Miki didn't begrudge the woman any of the money she was claiming, if anything she wanted to help with Michelle's medical expenses. And really, the house was too big for one woman to live in.

Miki yanked on the handle but the door didn't budge. She remembered the automatic locking system engaging as they'd driven away from their house but she was sure newer cars were fitted with a safety feature that meant you couldn't be locked in.

"I put the child lock on." She swung her gaze around to meet Grant's. "One of us will have to let you out and we're not doing that until we make one thing perfectly clear."

"You can run, Miki, but you can't hide." Dayne's voice held steely determination and sent a shiver down her spine. "We'll give you room but we're not walking away from this. From you. You can go hide in that big house of yours but you'll hear from us every day."

"But—"

"No buts, remember?" Grant reached over and brushed a fingertip down her cheek. "No holding back."

"I..."

"It's okay. We get that you need space. Hell, maybe we could do with some too. It's been a fast and furious weekend and I think we're all suffering from a little whiplash." Dayne laid his hand on her knee and squeezed gently. "But remember, no matter what time of day, if you want to talk, ring one of us. We're here for you whenever you need."

Miki didn't know what to say. On one hand, she wanted to stay with them, see where this thing between them could go. But on the other, she wanted to run as far and as fast as her legs would take her. It was the same scared feeling she'd had back in high school, and that just made her angry to think she hadn't matured from that frightened young girl.

Grant opened his door and climbed out. Miki waited tensely for him to let her out of the backseat but he didn't do it straight away. Instead, he stood there surveying her street. She tried to look at it as he would see it. A nice street full of homes where families lived. Young families. Old families. And, like her next door neighbour, elderly couples whose children had long since moved on to start their own lives elsewhere.

She sighed. There'd been so much hope and promise when they'd bought the house she'd now decided to sell. All empty pipe-dreams that never had a chance of coming true because the person she'd placed her trust in had betrayed her in the most basic of ways. Miki hadn't noticed Dayne get out of the car until he was standing at her open door offering her his hand. With trepidation, she placed her hand in his and allowed him to help her up.

"It'll be okay. I know you're feeling overwhelmed right now and you have every right to be, but we'll make this work. Whatever it takes." Dayne pulled her close and pressed his lips to hers.

His kiss wasn't anything like the numerous ones he'd given her over the weekend, but something about it had more effect than any of the passionate kisses he'd already lavished on her. He stepped back, smoothed the tip of his finger over her bottom lip and turned away. She watched him walk around the car and slip behind the steering wheel. He never looked back and Miki felt a painful twist in her chest.

Grant took her hand, entwined their fingers and softly caressed her palm with his thumb. She pulled her gaze from where Dayne had disappeared and turned to face Grant. He was studying their joined hands and she waited, giving him time to gather his thoughts. Besides, she still didn't know what to say.

"Dayne's right." He brought his gaze up to meet hers. "We'll make it work. Whatever it takes, however long it takes. That's a promise, Miki." Grant squeezed her fingers, brushed his lips on her cheek and let her go.

She watched as he climbed in the car and closed the door.

She stood in her driveway as Dayne started the engine and reversed out onto the street. She stared, unmoving, as they drove away until they turned the corner at the end of her street and disappeared from sight. Her shoulders sagged. The enormity of what she had to face hit her hard. Dread at having to deal with everything the house behind her meant, the house that had never really been home.

Miki turned and stared at the building behind her. So much had happened since she'd locked that door behind her on Friday night. The for-sale sign for one. It hadn't been there Friday or Saturday morning. The real estate woman must have come by sometime over the weekend. She'd said it would go on the market as of Monday. Seeing the big timber sign sticking out of the lawn made the decision real and gave Miki a churning sensation in the pit of her stomach, but whether that was from sadness or excitement at a new beginning she wasn't sure. One thing she was sure of was there was no putting it off. She had to go inside.

Using the spare key she picked up from Mrs Brimble, Miki let herself in the front door. Uneasy with the empty silence of the house, she flicked the stereo on as she walked through the lounge room. The air had a stale closed-off feel and she rushed around to open all the windows. As the breeze blew through, Miki breathed deep. Her phone and keys on the dining table caught her eye and she strode over to find a note from Frankie under them. In usual Frankie style, the note was short and to the point.

Dropped in. Ring me.

Miki wasn't up to talking to her best friend just yet. She needed to get a few things straight in her mind before she revealed anything to Frankie. Glancing at the wall clock, Miki noticed it wasn't even midday. A shower, some comfy clothes and a cup of coffee were what she wanted. In that order, but first she'd start the coffee machine so there'd be a fresh pot when she finished showering. But she never made it to coffee. As the water from the shower streamed over her, the dam burst and Miki sank to the floor and sobbed. She cried until the water ran cold, until the hard tiles made her arse numb and until there were no more tears to fall.

Violent shivers tore though her, shaking her from head to toe. Her fingers shook so badly that gripping the taps to turn the shower off proved difficult. Miki's eyes stung, her nose ran and her chest and stomach ached. Staggering out of the tub, she grabbed a towel and wrapped it around her shoulders. The trip to her bedroom resembled a drunken amble and she smashed her shin into the bed frame before collapsing onto the quilt. With her head buried in her pillow, Miki gave in to exhaustion.

GRANT WATCHED Dayne pace across the office again and clenched his fists. He was going to wear a hole in the floor and fall through it any second. His friend had alternated between pacing and sitting at his desk grumbling and it was starting to get on Grant's nerves. Saving the file he was working on, he shut down his computer and pushed back from his desk.

"I'm going for a run."

"What?" Dayne spun around to face him.

"You know, shorts, running shoes, walking fast?"

"I know what running is. What the hell do you think you're doing going for one? What if she rings?"

"Miki isn't ringing and you know it. In fact, I doubt we'll hear from her at all."

Dayne cursed and stormed over to his desk. With short jerky actions, he shoved the papers he'd pretended to work on back into their folder. "Dammit!" He flopped into his chair.

Grant walked to the door. "Burning off a bit of energy would be good for you. Get your gear on and meet me out front." He left the room without waiting for Dayne to acknowledge him, but he knew his friend would be waiting outside in a few minutes. It took him no time at all to strip down, pull on some shorts and his cross trainers. Noticing the haggard pair of shoes, Grant made a mental note to pick up a new pair soon.

They met at the door. Dayne engaged the alarm and they headed out. Taking their time to warm up, Grant wondered if he should say something, but he wasn't in the mood to talk and Dayne didn't seem inclined to either. By mutual agreement, they moved off the lawn out on to the footpath. Starting out slow, they built up speed and in minutes they were powering around the streets.

His heart rate elevated and sweat poured off him, but Grant kept going, kept pushing. Fire filled his chest as his lungs laboured to breathe and the heavy beat of his feet on concrete sounded like thunder. Every muscle burned, urging him to stop. Dayne ran beside him, straining as Grant was. It was punishment. Pain in the body took the focus off the pain in his heart, and he knew his mate was using their run to do the same. They rounded a bend and their place came into view again.

The sun was going down and dusk was rapidly turning into night. As they approached the house their pace slowed until they were walking. Dropping to the grass, Grant moved through a series of cool-down exercises. Each one killed and he winced in pain. *Shit.* He was going to be sorry tomorrow. Finished he got to his feet and looked at Dayne.

"We have to let her come to us."

"I know." His friend ran a hand over his face. "I want to go get her, drag her back here and never let her go, but I know that would be just as bad as getting down on my knees on her doorstep to beg her to come home."

"We can't make her come back, but that doesn't mean we can't try and convince her to."

"Want to flip a coin for who calls her first?"

Grant laughed. "No, you can, but I think we should leave her until tomorrow."

"Agreed."

"Come on, let's go in and pretend to work some more." Grant smiled, the first genuine one since they'd left Miki at her house. The one she was selling.

MIKI TUGGED the front of her shirt away from her sweaty breasts. She'd been dragging boxes from the shed into the house so she could endure the odious task of sorting through the last of David's things. Her own possessions had been dealt with over the last few months. Once she'd made the decision to sell the house she'd systematically gone through every drawer, every cupboard and tossed more than fifty percent of what she'd found.

So far there'd been nothing worth keeping in the shed, but these last few boxes held papers and photos which meant Miki would be going through them carefully. She figured most of what she'd find would be thrown out, but it was better to be safe now than sorry later. In the first box she found David's school papers. From report cards to certificates of achievement, it was a complete play-by-play of his school years. Miki packaged them back up, taped the top closed and used a permanent marker to write David's family in big letters across the side.

A sudden, strident ring disturbed the quiet of the house. Miki pushed back from the table and walked over to the wall that held the phone. She didn't need to look at caller ID to know who was on the other end of the line. Lifting the cradle she brought it to her ear.

"Hello."

"Hey, gorgeous."

"Hi, Dayne."

"How you doing?"

Miki rolled her eyes. "The same as I was an hour ago when Grant rang."

"Oh, Grant rang?"

She laughed. "You know he did, you're sitting next to him."

"Busted." She could hear the grin in his voice. "So, any chance you want to have dinner with us?"

Miki took a deep breath. She wasn't ready to see them again. She hadn't gotten around to sorting through her thoughts to know what to say if she did see them. There were other loose ends that needed tying off before she attempted to untangle what had happened last weekend.

"I'll take you silence as a no."

"Dayne."

"It's okay, Miki. I understand. I don't like it but I understand it."

"Thank you."

"For what? Pestering you every few hours?"

"No. For being so patient with me while I..." Miki couldn't think of how to explain what she was doing or why. "Sort myself out?"

"Is that what you're doing?"

"Yeah. I'm going through my old life. I can't even begin to live in this one until I put the old one to rest."

"That's why you're selling the house?"

"Partly."

"You'll ring if you need us?"

"Yes."

"Good then. I'll let you get back to it."

"Bye."

"Bye, I love you."

Dayne hung up before she could utter a sound. He did it every time. You would think she'd get a clue and say something before he ended his calls with that final line, but she didn't. She knew why he did it. One thing about Dayne that appealed to her was his intelligence. It was just a shame he was using that smart mind to get at her. Declaring his love like that meant it was the last thing she heard whenever he rang, guaranteeing she'd be thinking about it for ages after.

Miki hung up the receiver and went back to the dining table. Not that it really bothered her to hear him say he loved her. No, what bothered her was that it made her miss him. Miss them and all they were offering. With a sigh, she plonked down in her chair. Five days without seeing them. Five days of continuous phone calls that should have driven her batty. Instead she lived for those scant few minutes where she got to hear one of their voices. *Damn.* She was so screwed up. And probably screwing up the best thing that ever happened to her into the bargain.

She dragged the next box closer to her chair and leaned over to pull the top photo album out. Her breath caught when the album below was revealed. A white embossed leather cover with gold script, an intricate pattern around the edges and a couple entwined on a love seat in the centre. Her wedding album. Miki traced the fancy design with a fingertip. So much lay hidden under the cover. So many dreams and hopes that had never seen the light of day. So many lies. So much deceit.

With trembling fingers, Miki picked up the album and, like it was a bomb about to explode, placed it gingerly on the table. The other albums were forgotten as she stared at that white cover now dull with age. It still felt soft under her fingertips.

The leather, although in need of care, had stood the test of time and neglect. She couldn't remember the last time she'd seen the photos inside. Couldn't remember packing it away.

Reaching over for the dust rag, Miki carefully brushed the thin layer coating the album. She wasn't sure how she felt about looking inside, but she knew she was going to. Lifting the cover to reveal the first page, she held her breath. What did it say about her that she couldn't remember what picture would greet her? Her fingertips lightly traced the black and white shot. She and David running through the tunnel of bubbles their guests were blowing over them. The picture had been her favourite. How had she forgotten that?

The next few pages were her and her bridesmaids getting ready. She laughed at the look on Frankie's face. They'd had so much fun getting their hair and make-up done, pulling on their dresses. Miki studied the shot of her and Frankie admiring the beading in Miki's gown. The memory of that day came flooding back, Frankie bitching about the silly froufrou skirt and the girly peach colour. For all her protesting, she'd been a knockout in that dress. Her friend had been willing to do anything for her even though she'd hated the groom-to-be.

Miki frowned. Frankie had hated David with a passion, and at first she'd been upset that her future husband and best friend didn't get along. But it had quickly become apparent that Frankie and David were happy to ignore each other as much as possible and be pleasant when they couldn't. She had to wonder why Frankie had never said, "I told you so," when things had started to unravel between her and David. Her best friend had lived up to the title by being everything Miki had needed every step of the way. Especially during the hard last few years of her marriage and then when David had gotten himself killed and the woman with him badly injured.

She turned another page and stared at the picture taken

minutes after she and David had spoken their vows. Happiness radiated off the young woman in the arms of her new husband. Miki remembered being so happy, deliriously happy. But David...he looked happy enough, but the smile didn't quite reach his eyes and he seemed to be holding her awkwardly as though he were uncomfortable. Miki looked closer. Why had she never noticed the strained edge to him before?

He'd always been happiest in the limelight, and yet in this picture it was like he couldn't wait for it to be over so he could move away. Miki's stomach rolled. She quickly flipped over another page and examined the photos carefully. The bridal party, everyone pressed together so they could all fit in, but David was angled away from her while she leaned into him smiling a dazzling white smile. Another picture, another tense embrace. Her stomach clenched.

Why had she never taken notice before? Had her complete joy over her wedding overshadowed her groom's unhappiness? Because that's what he was, unhappy. In every picture, on every page, on his face, in his eyes, his body language said he wasn't happy. How could she miss that? Miki pushed the album aside, picked up a different one. This one held snapshots of their honeymoon. Again, there was stiffness in David's embrace, but he did seem happy, at least his eyes were smiling in these pictures.

She flicked through page after page, album after album. Each one showing their lives until the last one held mainly scenery, the odd snap of her or him, but none of them together. The last photo was taken two years before David's death. When had she stopped documenting their adventures? Staring up at her was David, the angry creases in his forehead, the frown on his lips and the fire shooting from his eyes. He hadn't wanted her at the off-road racing gala day. He'd been furious when she'd shown up. It wouldn't be until two years later that she would understand why.

Michelle had been there, one of the sponsor's promo girls. It all made perfect sense. His disinterest in going places with her, the way he'd withheld information about where he was going, what he was doing. Miki closed her eyes, squeezed them tight against the pain lancing her temple, her heart. It had all been a lie. Every last day of her life was a lie. Tears flowed down her face, dripped from her chin. She'd thrown away her dreams and hopes on a man who'd never had an interest in catching them. In making them real.

Miki shoved away from the table, swept the albums to the floor and stared at the jumbled mess she'd made.

"Oh God," she groaned, and bent at the waist as her stomach cramped. "What have I done?"

She stood up, turned around. Took a step. Stopped. Turned back. Miki lashed out, kicked the photo album closest to her. Pain shot through her big toe and into her foot, but she didn't care. Pain was real. She kicked out again. And again. Stomping on the pictures that couldn't hide the truth. Jumping up and down, she smashed the white album, tearing the leather with her rage. Then she stopped as suddenly as she'd begun and gasped.

Spinning on her heel, she ran from the room. "I have to go." Miki searched for her shoes and keys. She'd wasted years on a relationship that never stood a chance and yet she'd been willing to walk away from one that felt as right as breathing just because it wasn't *normal*. "Stupid."

Purse in hand and flip-flops on her feet, Miki raced out the door.

8

DAYNE STOPPED what he was doing and stared down the hall. "Who the fuck could that be?" He wasn't expecting an answer. Grant was in the other room. Tossing the dishcloth on the counter, he strode towards the front door as the doorbell rang again.

"Yeah, yeah, hold your horses."

"Who's that?" Grant met him in the foyer.

"How would I know, I haven't opened the fucking door yet," he barked.

Grant stepped aside and held up his hands.

"Sorry, man." Dayne sighed and wrapped his hand around the door knob. "It's been five days and I'm starting to get a litt —Mikaila?"

"I'm sorry. I should have called, I should have—"

"No, what you should do is get your arse in this house right now." Grant reached past Dayne to grip Miki's forearm and yank her over the threshold.

As soon as she'd cleared the door Dayne slammed it shut. He turned to find Miki standing there, with her head slightly bowed and her hands twisting together at her waist, her knuckles turning white. Dayne couldn't think of what to say. The urge to take her in his arms was strong, but he was terrified she wasn't real. That his stressed-out, frustrated psyche had conjured her up, and if he touched her she'd disappear in a puff of smoke.

"I shouldn't have come without calling."

"No, you shouldn't have left." Dayne regretted the words the second they left his mouth. "I'm sorry, but I've been going out of my mind not seeing you."

She looked up, their gazes connected and he saw hope shining in her blue eyes. "You have?"

"Oh yeah, totally out of his mind." Grant took a step forward but didn't touch her again. "And mine."

"Oh God, I'm so sorry. I'll go." She turned to leave and Dayne moved to block her way.

"Hell, no. You're not going anywhere."

Miki gasped and stepped back. "But—"

"There you go with the buts again," Grant said.

"Why are you here, Miki?" Dayne asked.

"I um, well, I was looking at photos." Her tongue darted out to wet her lips. "And well, he wasn't happy and I was and I never knew. How could I not know?"

She made no sense, but Dayne didn't have time to question her because words just kept falling out of her mouth.

"I wanted things, things he was never going to be able to give me, and yet I married him anyway because I didn't know, and Frankie never liked him and she was right about him in so many ways, but never once did she say 'I told you so' and doesn't that make her the best best friend ever?"

Did she even breathe? Dayne shook his head. Tried to clear the fog and make sense of anything that had spewed from her mouth.

"The truth is I still want those things. Love, marriage, house, babies, the whole deal. I didn't think I did, but I do. And I want them here, with you, both of you, if you'll have me. I don't know how we'd make it work or if I haven't screwed everything up... I have, haven't I? God, I've screwed it up."

"Whoa. I have no idea what you've just said. The only thing I got was you wanted to be here with us."

"Is that what you're saying? You want to be with us?" Grant asked.

Miki took a deep breath and let it out slowly. "I dare you to give me another chance."

"Dare?" Dayne laughed. "Miki, honey, you had me the minute you showed up on the doorstep, no dare necessary." He still kept his distance because the second he touched her she'd be minus her clothes and he'd be sliding inside her tight warm body with the erection he'd sported since opening the door.

"I did?" Her eyes crinkled and her nose scrunched up. "Really?"

"You still don't believe we're in this for the long haul? After last weekend? All the phone calls this week?" Grant reached out to brush the hair from her eyes. "But here's the deal, Miki, we'll take your dare but you have to play the game too. No holding back. Nothing but the truth about everything, good and bad."

She nodded and the tightness in Dayne's chest eased. "Truth *and* dare, Miki?"

Spin The Bottle

By Rhian Cahill

The only rule is the rules always change

Modelling gave Lillian McDermott amazing experiences and enough money to leave it all behind to start her own perfume and fashion label, but it didn't give her the man she's always loved—Mackenzie Harris.

Her brother's best friend, Mac only sees her as a surrogate little sister, except Lillian's success wasn't handed to her. She knows what it means to work hard and she intends to use the same single-minded intensity to rock Mac's world until ignoring her is impossible.

Best mates don't screw around with little sisters so no matter how tempting Mackenzie Harris finds Lillian McDermott it's hands off. That doesn't mean he's ever been immune to her charms.

With one spin of the bottle Lilli turns up the heat and Mac's not one to back down from a challenge. And once that line is crossed, there's no turning back.

Note: A game of Spin the Bottle is hell on one's self control.

http://www.rhiancahill.com/books/party-games/spin-the-bottle/

Each player, one after the other, took a card. All of them went above twenty-one and took a shot. A second round started up quickly and Lil stood off to the side to watch. She was enjoying the game when someone pressed into the back of her. Thinking the person wanted to get past, she stepped forward only to be stopped by an arm around her waist, a strong grip that pulled her back against the solid hot wall of muscle behind her.

Warm air fanned over her ear and neck, sending shivers down her spine. His scent filled her nose, and he didn't need to speak for Lil to know who had hold of her. Mac. He gripped her hip, splayed his fingers and urged her to take a step backwards. Her body was never her own when he was around, and she let him lead her where he willed. He moved them out of the way and stepped them into the corner of the room.

In a second, Mac spun her around. He pushed her into the corner and caged her in, his hands flat on the wall either side of her waist. In her five-inch heels they were eye to eye and she could see the swirl of emotion in his blue gaze. She'd gone too far with tonight's party, but that wasn't what had her worried. No, what made her anxious was the look on his face that said he wanted to kiss her. They'd been there and done that with disastrous effects. Lillian didn't know if she could survive a second time.

"You can run, Lilli, but you can't hide forever."

Mac waited for the explosion. He didn't for one second think she'd let him get away with pinning her in a corner. No, Lillian McDermott never let anyone limit her. She took what she wanted when she wanted. It galled him to think she'd turned out exactly like her mother. That woman had a lot to answer for, the least of which was her absentee parenting. He shuddered. The last person he wanted occupying his mind was Gabriella McDermott. He'd much rather concentrate on her sexy daughter.

The one who drove him nuts but pulled him closer with every breath he took. He'd tried to stay away, tried to ignore the gut-burning need to see if the kiss they'd shared was a fluke. His gaze dropped to her mouth. Slightly parted, her cherry-red lips beckoned, a siren's call he knew he couldn't refuse—didn't want to deny. Mac leaned forward, his lips a breath from hers.

"Mac?"

His name on her tongue, the puff of warm air that blew over his chin and the tremor of her lips made him smile. "Lilli."

"What are you doing?" she whispered.

"I thought that was obvious." He didn't pull away but moved his body closer to hers, his chest barely touching the tips of her breasts when she sucked in a breath.

"You can't."

"Can't?"

"N-no." Her lips brushed his. "It's bad, remember?"

Mac pulled back a fraction to focus on her eyes. "What?"

"Kissing me." She licked her lips and sent his blood pressure soaring. "When we did it before, you said it was bad."

For a second, he hadn't a clue what she meant, and then it clicked. "Oh, no, it wasn't the kiss that was bad, Lilli." He lowered his head, brought his mouth back within touching distance of hers. "I'll prove it."

He slanted his mouth across hers. Thrust his tongue between her parted lips to plunder. Mac didn't ease into the kiss. He dove deep, headfirst. She tasted of champagne and cherries. Of lush decadence that spoke of untold pleasure. The party faded away, lost in the mating of their mouths. Nothing existed but the woman now in his arms, her body plastered to his, her soft curves cradling his hard edges as he devoured her.

Her breath hitched when he sucked on her tongue, and the gaspy little moan that followed the caress of his hand down her spine dragged him further into the most sublime kiss of his life.

Rhian Cahill is the alter ego of a former stay-at-home mother of four. With motherly duties rapidly dwindling Rhian is able to make use of the fertile imagination she used to keep herself sane for all those years of slavery. Having spent years living overseas and visiting tropical climates has helped inspire some steamy stories.

Multi-published in erotic romance and contemporary romance, Rhian, with the help of Mr. Muse, spends her days and nights writing.

When not glued to the keyboard you'll find her book or knitting in hand avoiding any and all housework as much as possible.

For more on Rhian –

Website – http://www.rhiancahill.com/

Newsletter signup – http://www.rhiancahill.com/contact/newsletter/

Reader group - https://www.facebook.com/groups/211469429208895/

Twitter – https://twitter.com/RhianCahill

FaceBook – https://www.facebook.com/RhianCahillAuthor

Instagram – http://instagram.com/rhiancahill/

BookBub – https://www.bookbub.com/authors/rhian-cahill

Goodreads page - https://www.goodreads.com/rhian_cahill

LOOK FOR THESE TITLES BY RHIAN CAHILL

Doing Logan

Shut Up And Kiss Me

Secret Confessions: Sydney Housewives – Virginia

Boys Of Summer

Bondi Beach Boys

Sand, Surf And Sunnie

Holiday Romances

Christmas Wishes

New Year's Kisses

Valentine's Dates

Secret Santa

Passport To Passion Collection

One Night In Bangkok

Singapore Fling

Coyote Hunger Series

Coyote Home – Book 1

Coyote Wild – Book 2

Coyote Whispers – Book 3

Coyote Law – Book 3.5

Coyote Lies – Book 4

Only You Series

All Of You – Book 1

Party Games Series

Truth Or Dare

Spin The Bottle

Pass The Parcel – Novella

Are You Game Series

7 Minutes In Heaven – Book 1

Catch'n'Kiss – Book 2

Red Light, Green Light – Book 3

Frosty's Snowmen Series

A Touch Of Frost

A Kiss From Kringle

A Taste For Kandy

Hearts Are Wild Series

No More Talking (novella)

Dare You To (novella)

Mad Love

Winter Lake Series

Love Me Like You Do

Love The Way You Are

When You Love Someone

Let me Love You

Wild Rush Of Love

For a full list of Rhian's available books visit her website

http://www.rhiancahill.com/books/